BROBOTS™

AND THE MECHA MALARKEY!

ONI PRESS

ONI
PRESS
PRESENTS

BRO

AND TH

EDITED BY
JAMES LUCAS JONES

BOTs

MECHA MALARKEY!

WRITTEN BY
J. TORRES

ART, LETTERING,
& DESIGN BY
SEAN DOVE

PUBLISHED BY ONI PRESS, INC.

JOE NOZEMACK, PUBLISHER
JAMES LUCAS JONES, EDITOR IN CHIEF
DAVID DISSANAYAKE, SALES MANAGER
RACHEL REED, PUBLICITY COORDINATOR
TROY LOOK, DIRECTOR OF DESIGN & PRODUCTION
HILARY THOMPSON, GRAPHIC DESIGNER
ANGIE DOBSON, DIGITAL PREPRESS TECHNICIAN
ARI YARWOOD, MANAGING EDITOR
CHARLIE CHU, SENIOR EDITOR
ROBIN HERRERA, EDITOR
ALISSA SALLAH, ADMINISTRATIVE ASSISTANT
BRAD ROOKS, DIRECTOR OF LOGISTICS
JUNG LEE, LOGISTICS ASSOCIATE

ONIPRESS.COM

ONIPRESS.COM
FACEBOOK.COM/ONIPRESS
TWITTER.COM/ONIPRESS
ONIPRESS.TUMBLR.COM
INSTAGRAM.COM/ONIPRESS

Find J. TORRES online at

FACEBOOK.COM/JTORRESCOMICS
@JTORRESCOMICS

Find SEAN DOVE online at

ANDTHANKYOUFORFLYING.COM
@ANDTHANKYOU

FIRST EDITION: AUGUST 2017

ISBN 978-1-62010-424-8
EISBN 978-1-62010-425-5

PRINTED IN SINGAPORE

LIBRARY OF CONGRESS CONTROL NUMBER: 2017932344

1 2 3 4 5 6 7 8 9 10

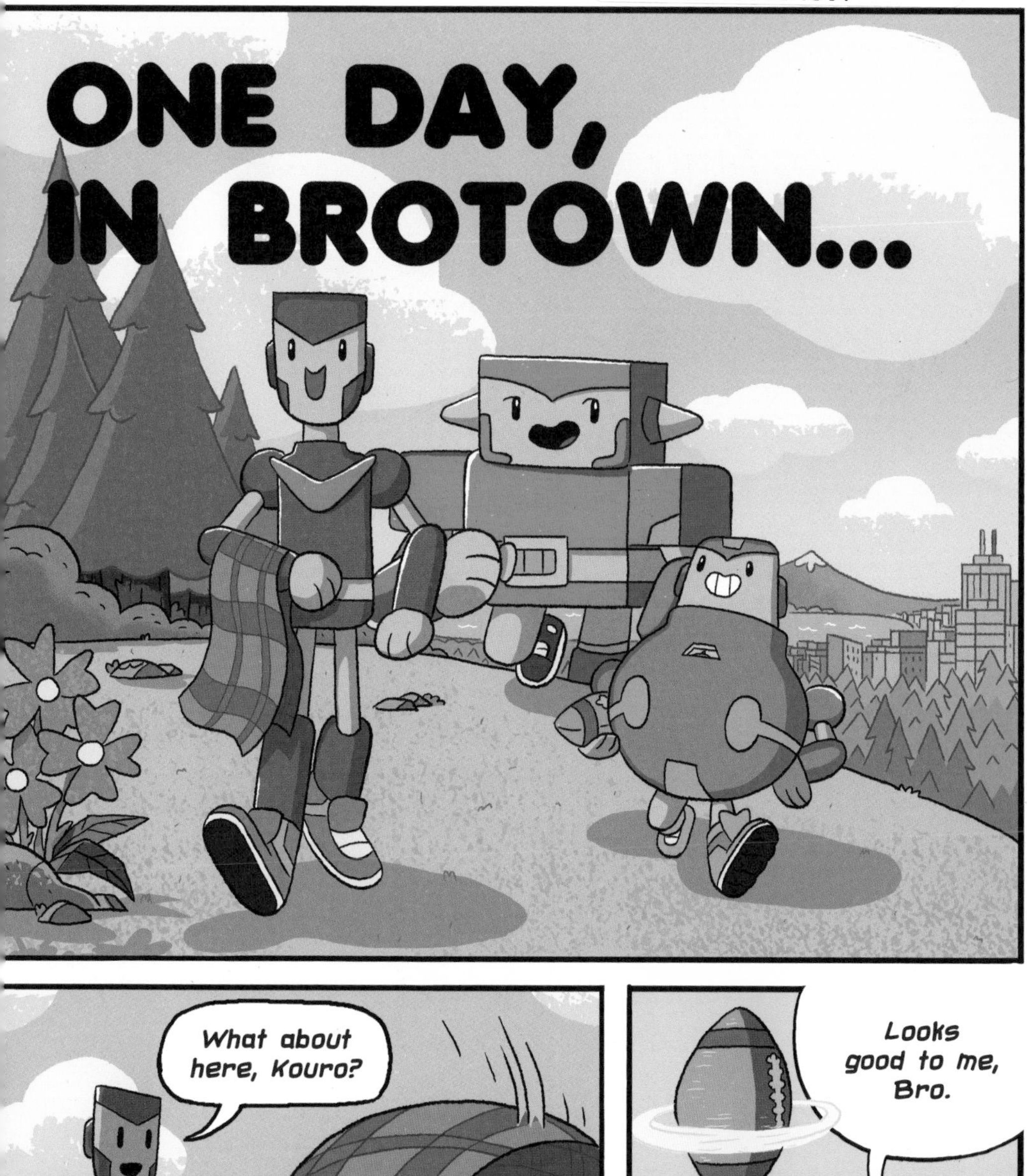
ONE DAY, IN BROTOWN...

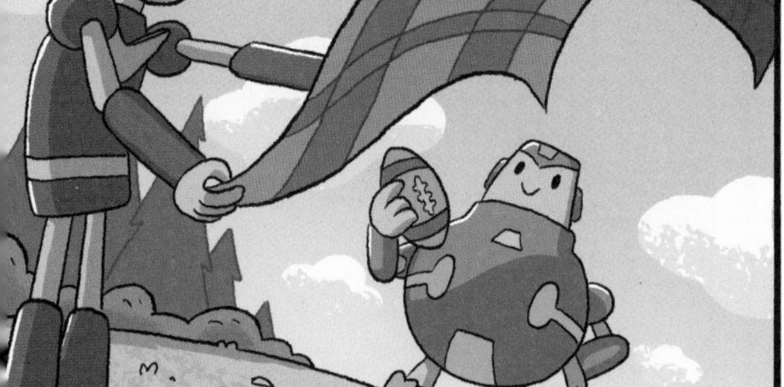
What about here, Kouro?

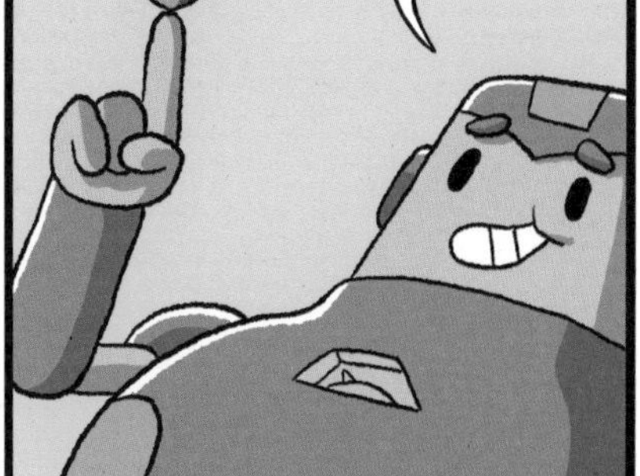
Looks good to me, Bro.

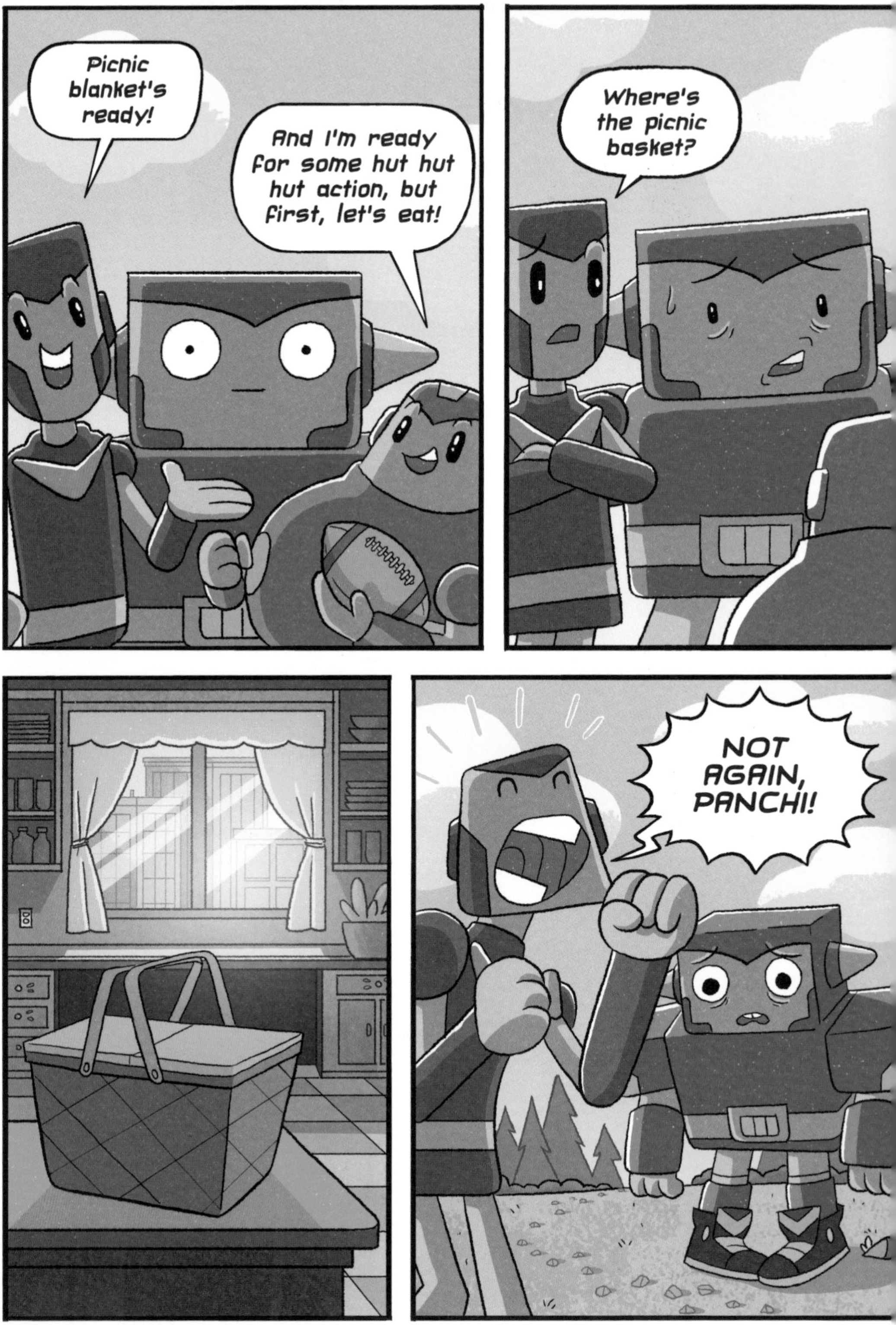

Picnic blanket's ready!
And I'm ready for some hut hut hut action, but first, let's eat!
Where's the picnic basket?
NOT AGAIN, PANCHI!

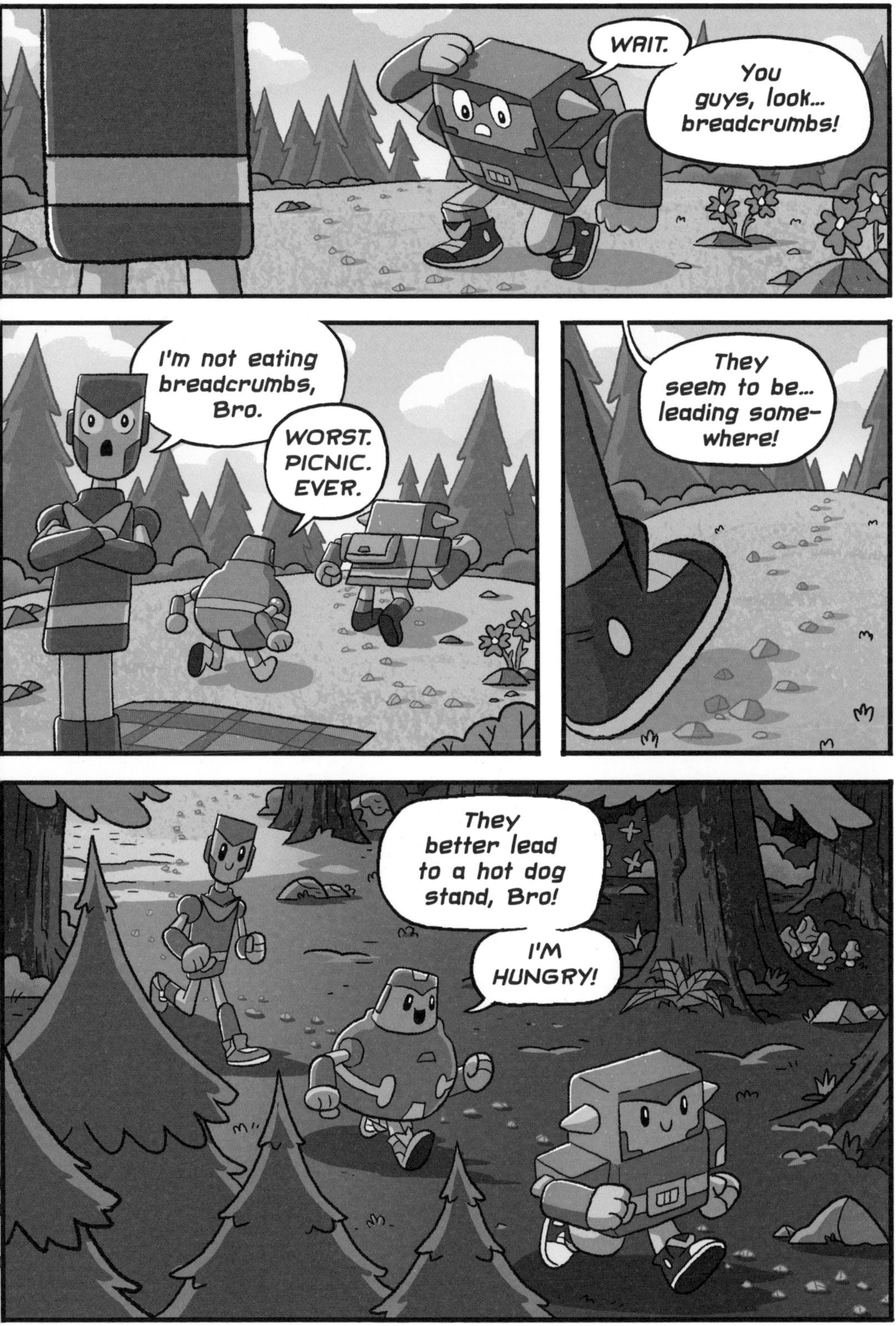
WAIT.
You guys, look... breadcrumbs!
I'm not eating breadcrumbs, Bro.
WORST. PICNIC. EVER.
They seem to be... leading some-where!
They better lead to a hot dog stand, Bro!
I'M HUNGRY!

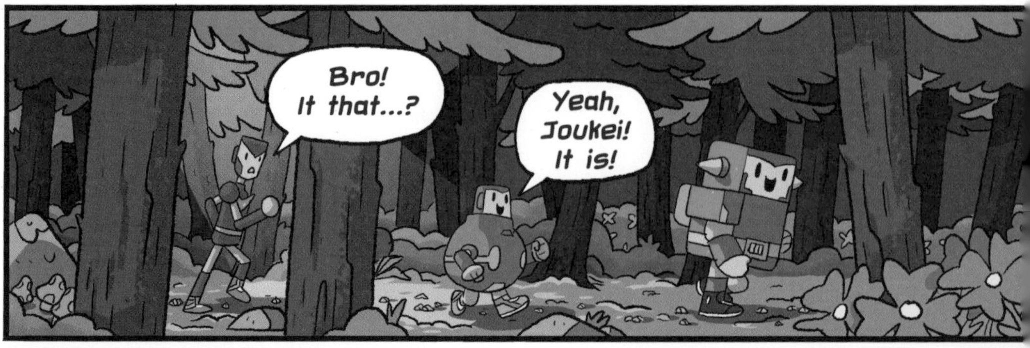
Bro!
It that...?
Yeah, Joukei! It is!

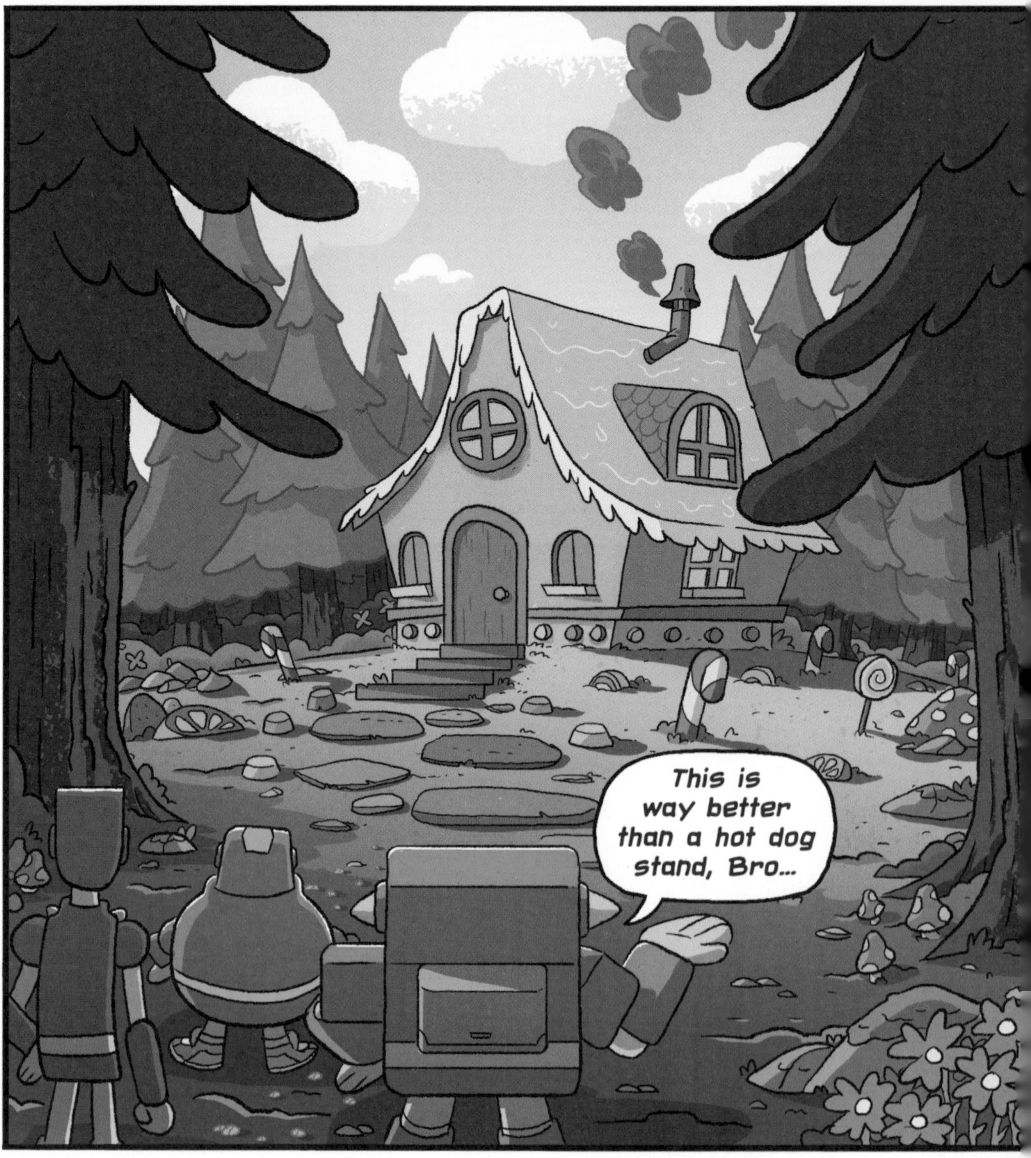
This is way better than a hot dog stand, Bro...

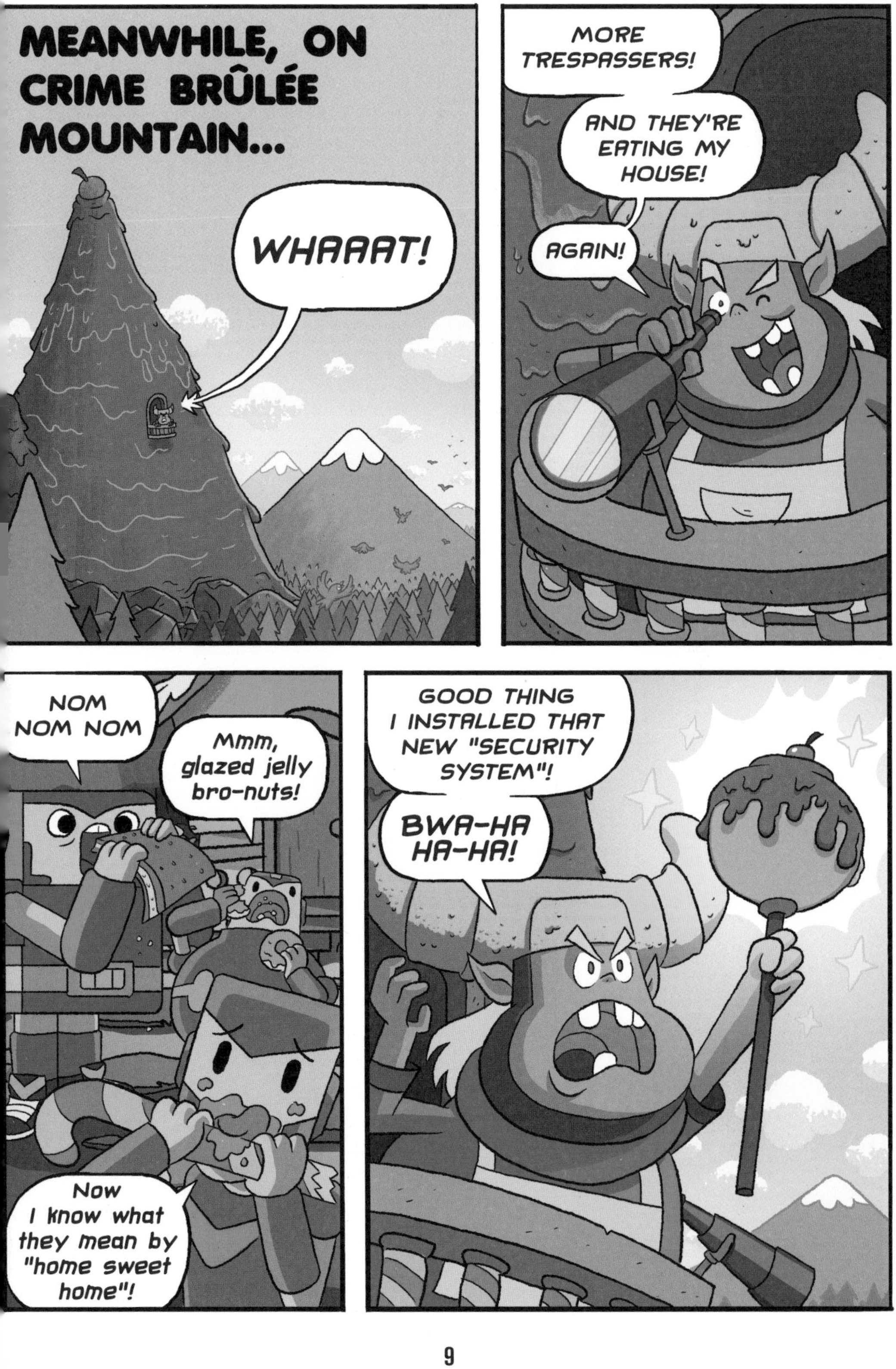
MEANWHILE, ON CRIME BRÛLÉE MOUNTAIN...
WHAAAT!
MORE TRESPASSERS!
AND THEY'RE EATING MY HOUSE!
AGAIN!
NOM NOM NOM
Mmm, glazed jelly bro-nuts!
Now I know what they mean by "home sweet home"!
GOOD THING I INSTALLED THAT NEW "SECURITY SYSTEM"!
BWA-HA HA-HA!

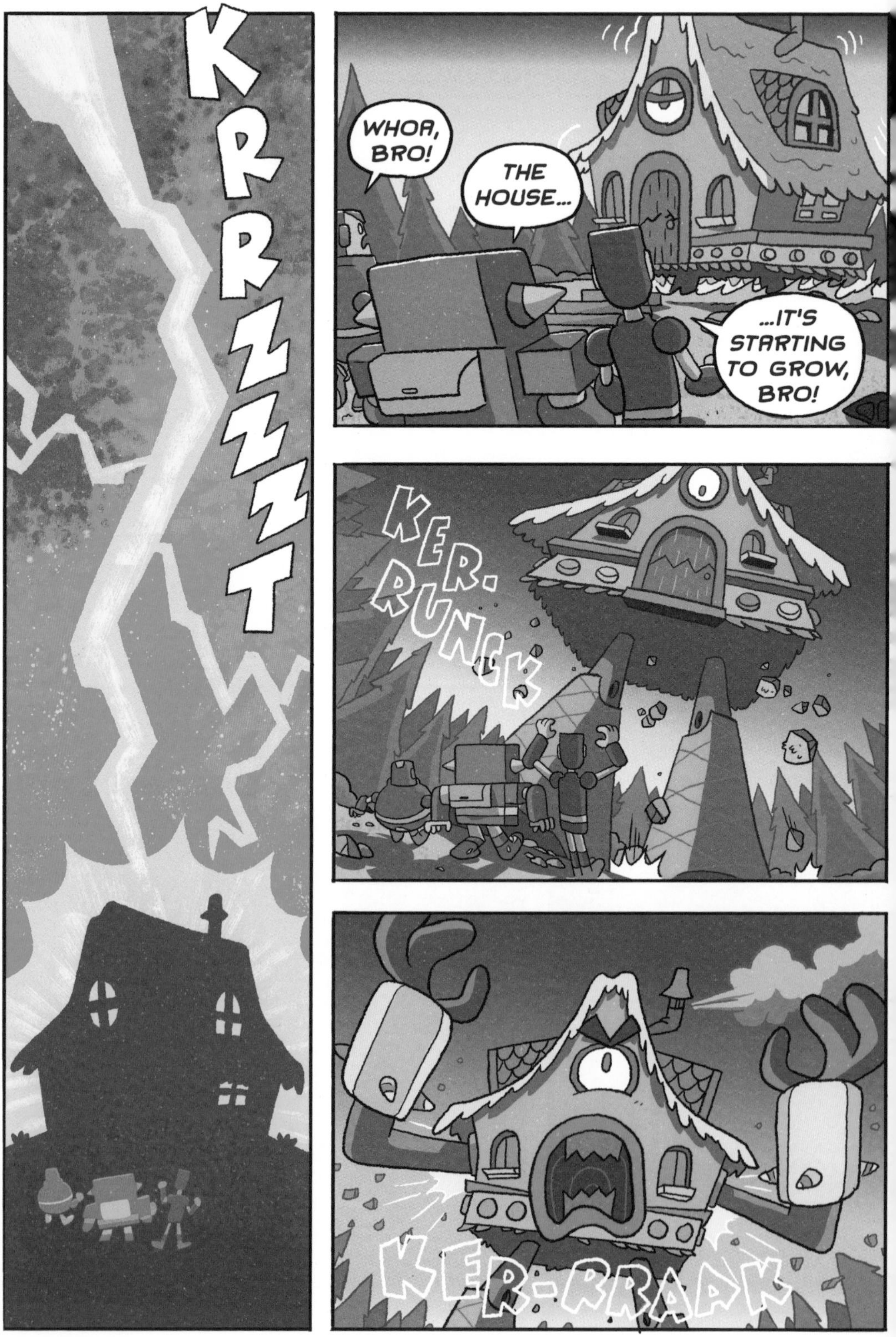
KRRZZZZT
WHOA, BRO!
THE HOUSE...
...IT'S STARTING TO GROW, BRO!
KER-RUNCK
KER-RRAAK

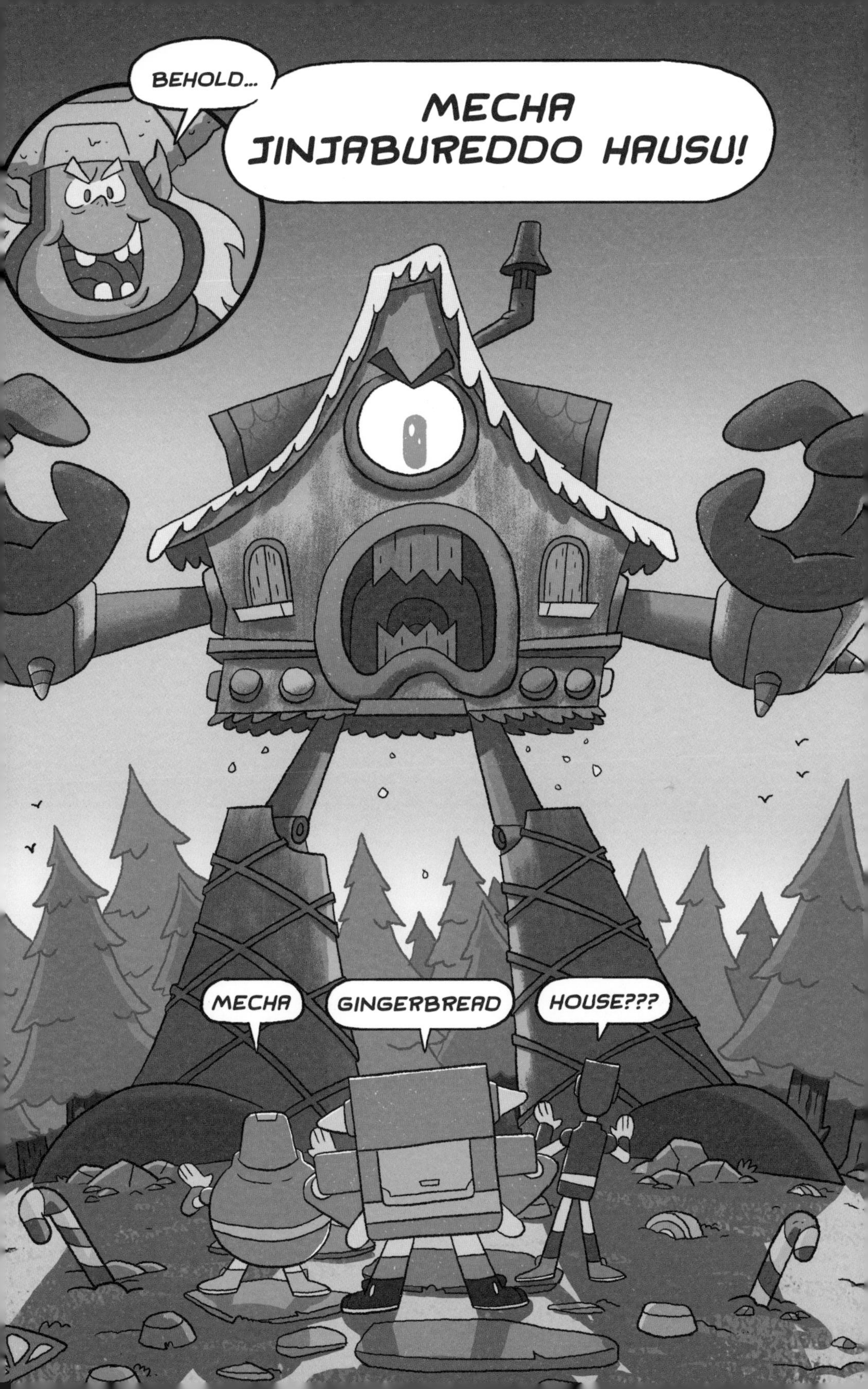
BEHOLD...
MECHA JINJABUREDDO HAUSU!
MECHA
GINGERBREAD
HOUSE???

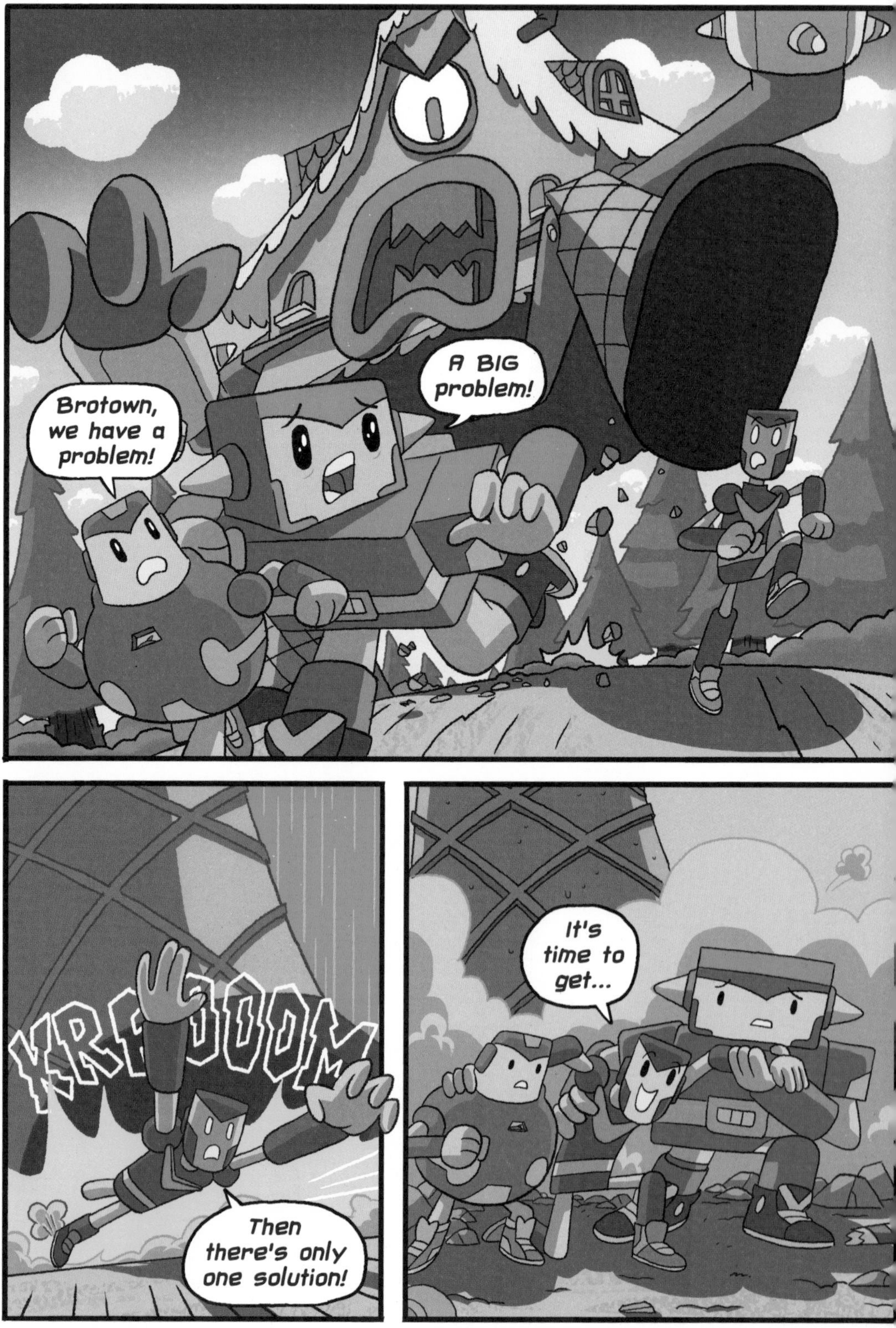
Brotown, we have a problem!
A BIG problem!
Then there's only one solution!
It's time to get...

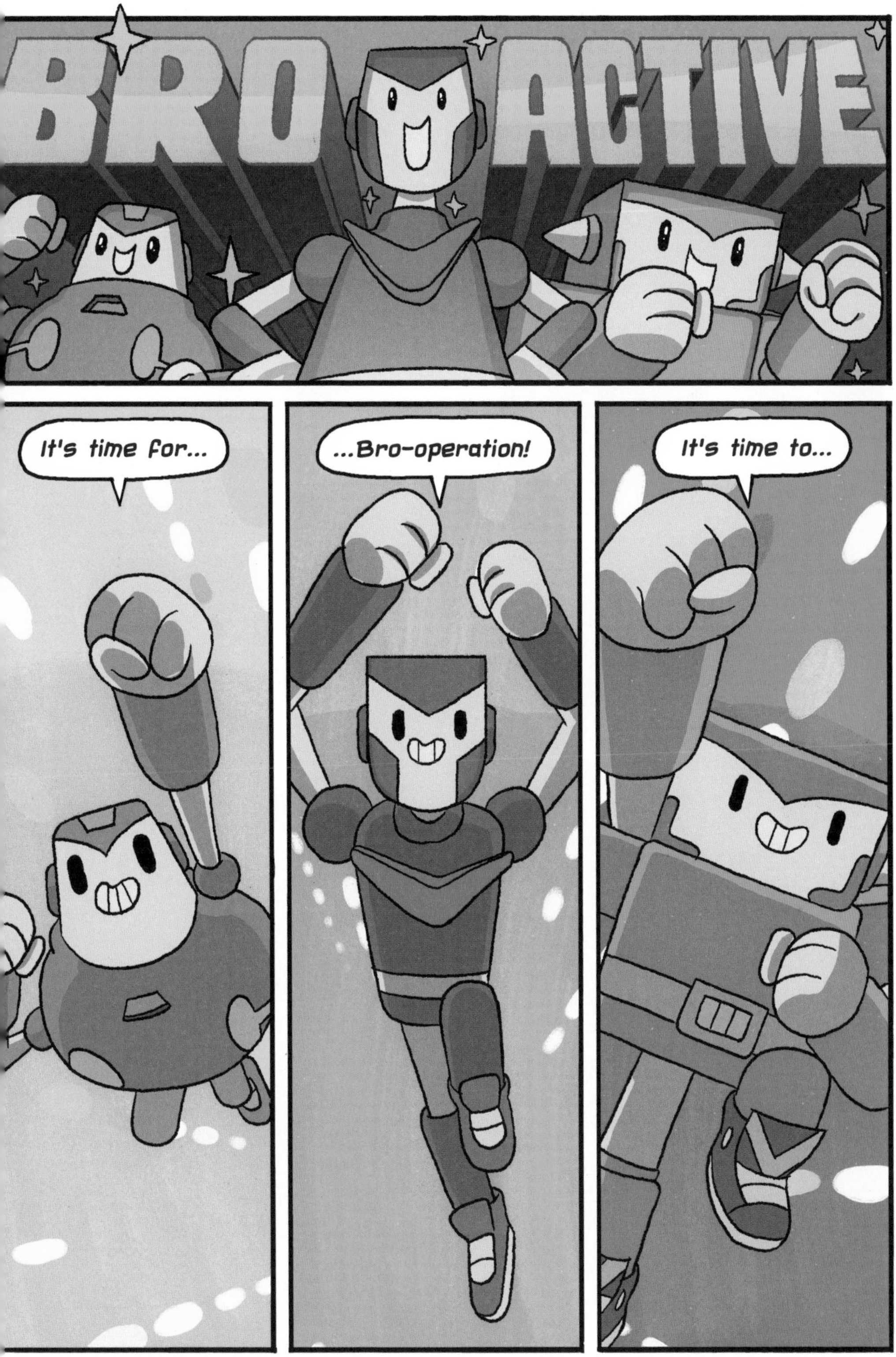
BRO-ACTIVE
It's time for...
...Bro-operation!
It's time to...

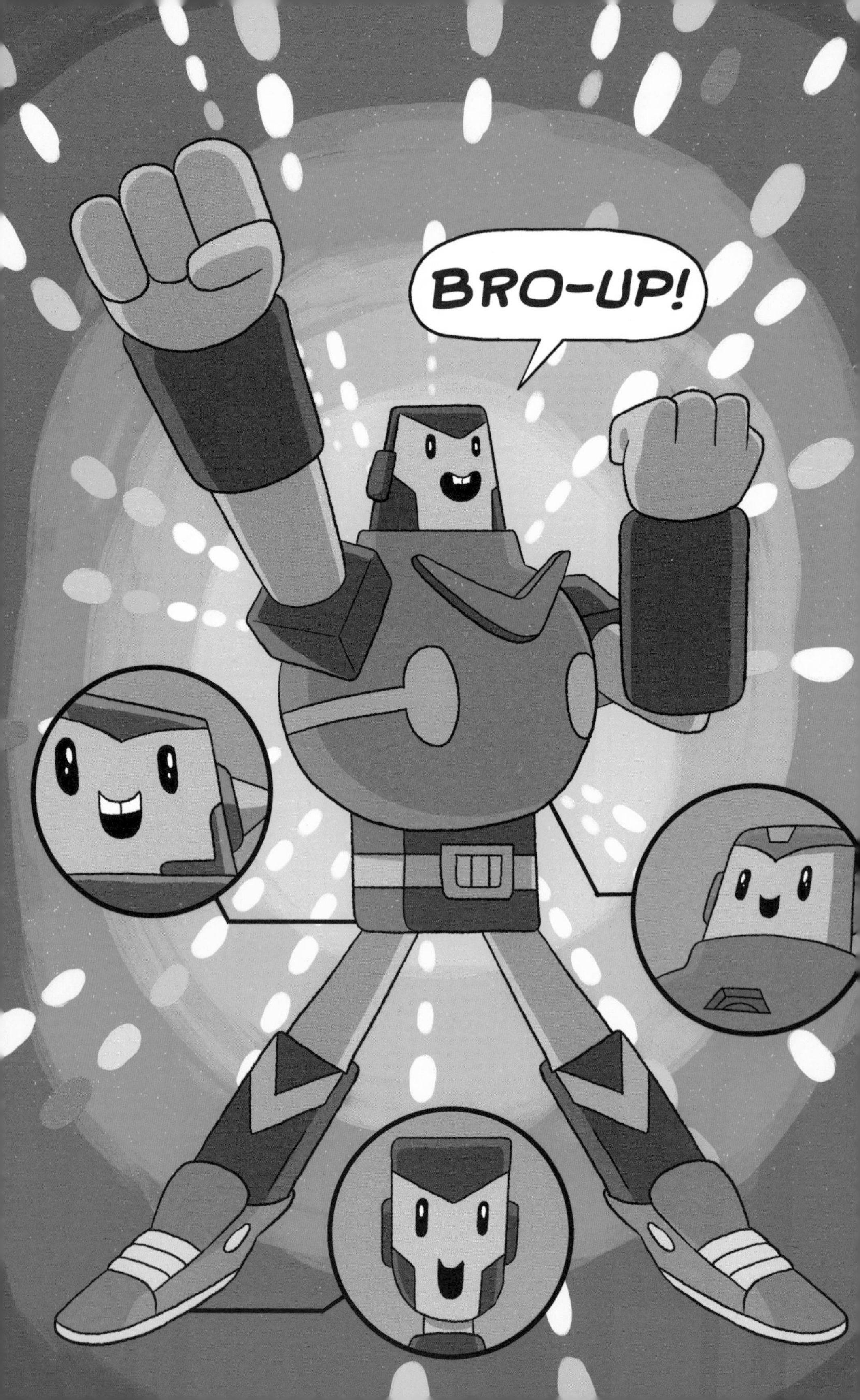
BRO-UP!

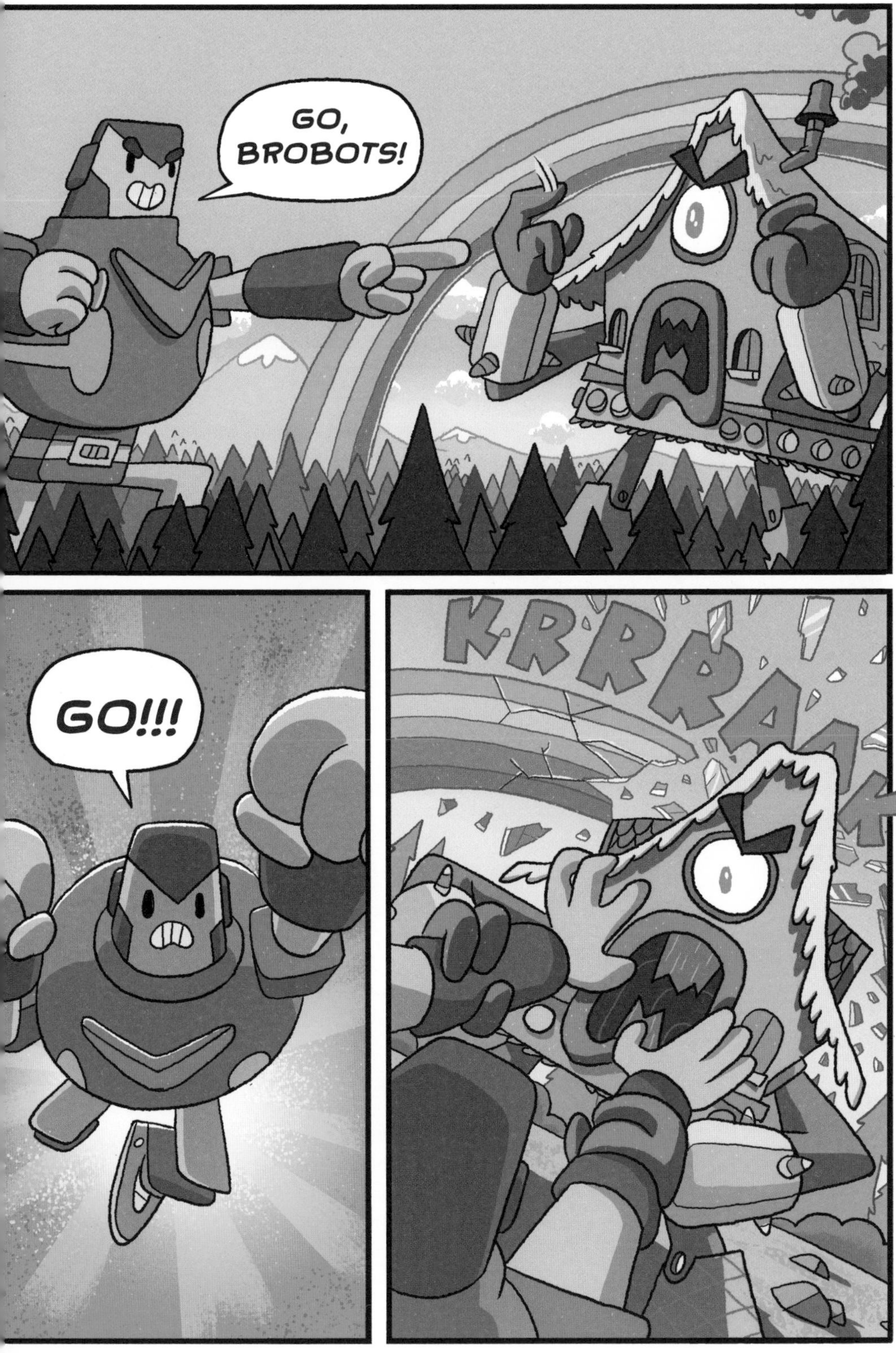
GO, BROBOTS!
GO!!!
KRRRAAK

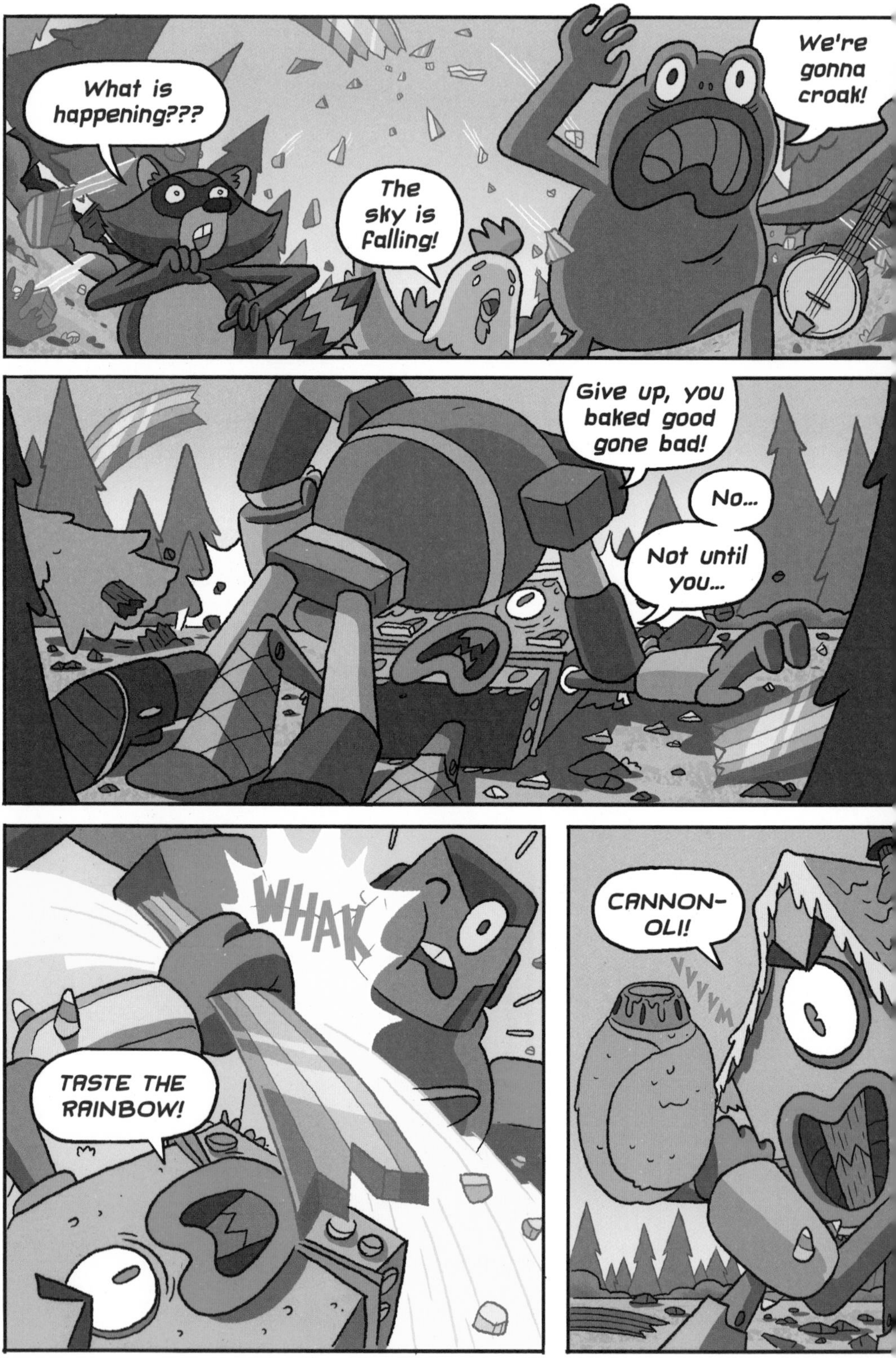
What is happening???
The sky is falling!
We're gonna croak!
Give up, you baked good gone bad!
No...
Not until you...
WHAK
TASTE THE RAINBOW!
CANNON-OLI!
VVVVM

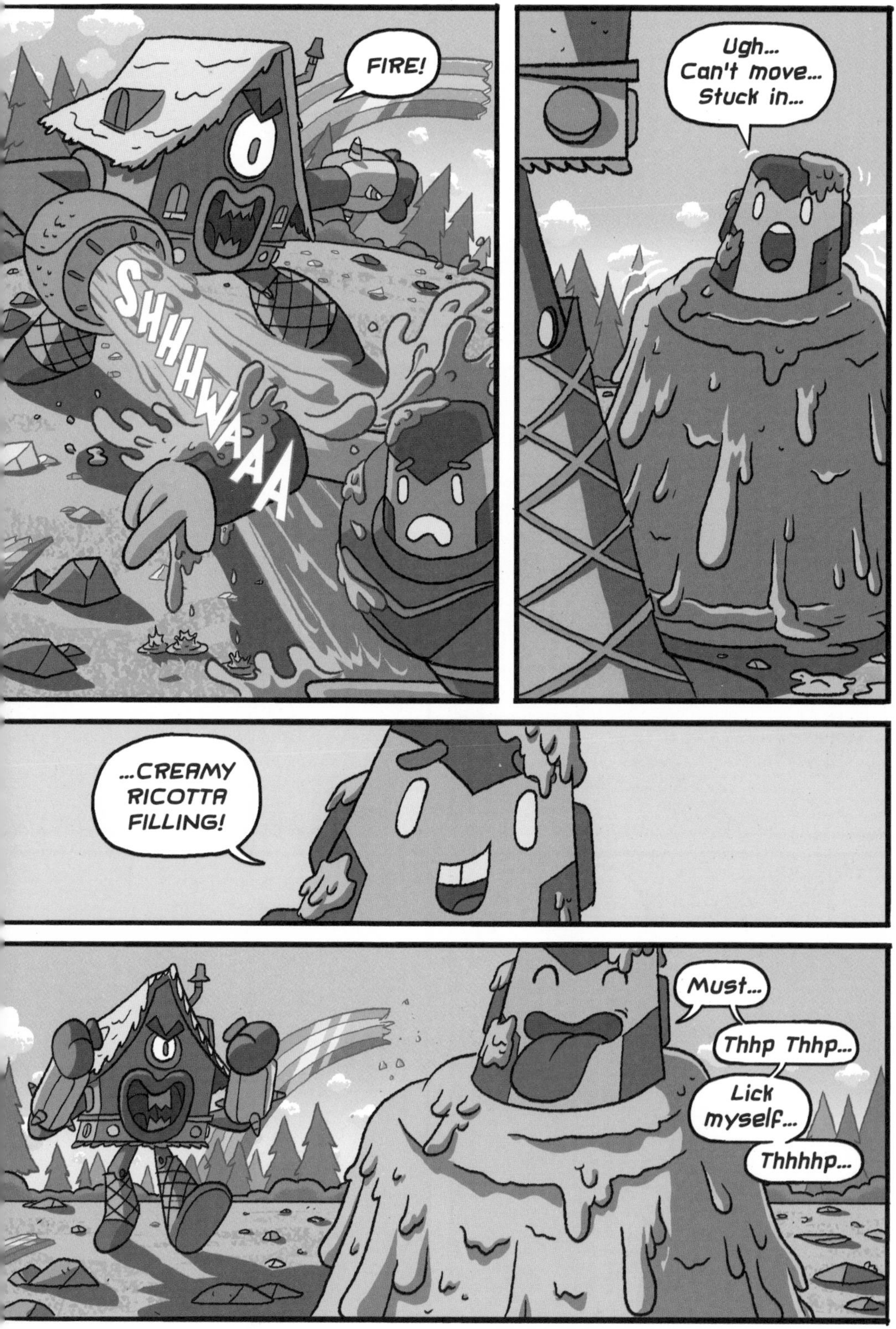
FIRE!
SHHHWAAAA
Ugh... Can't move... Stuck in...
...CREAMY RICOTTA FILLING!
Must...
Thhp Thhp...
Lick myself...
Thhhhp...

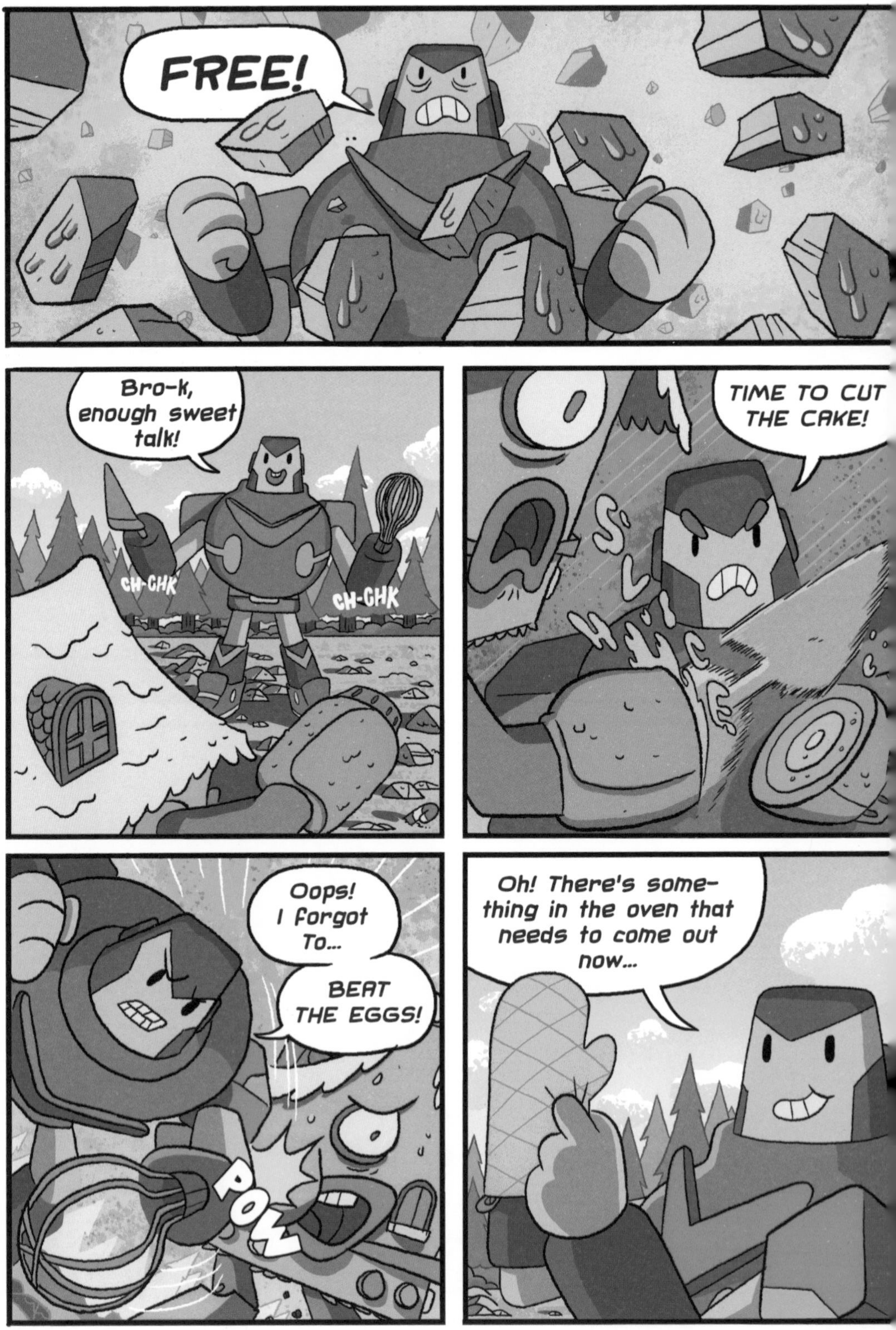
FREE!
Bro-k, enough sweet talk!
CH-CHK
CH-CHK
TIME TO CUT THE CAKE!
SLICE
Oops! I forgot To...
BEAT THE EGGS!
POW
Oh! There's some-thing in the oven that needs to come out now...

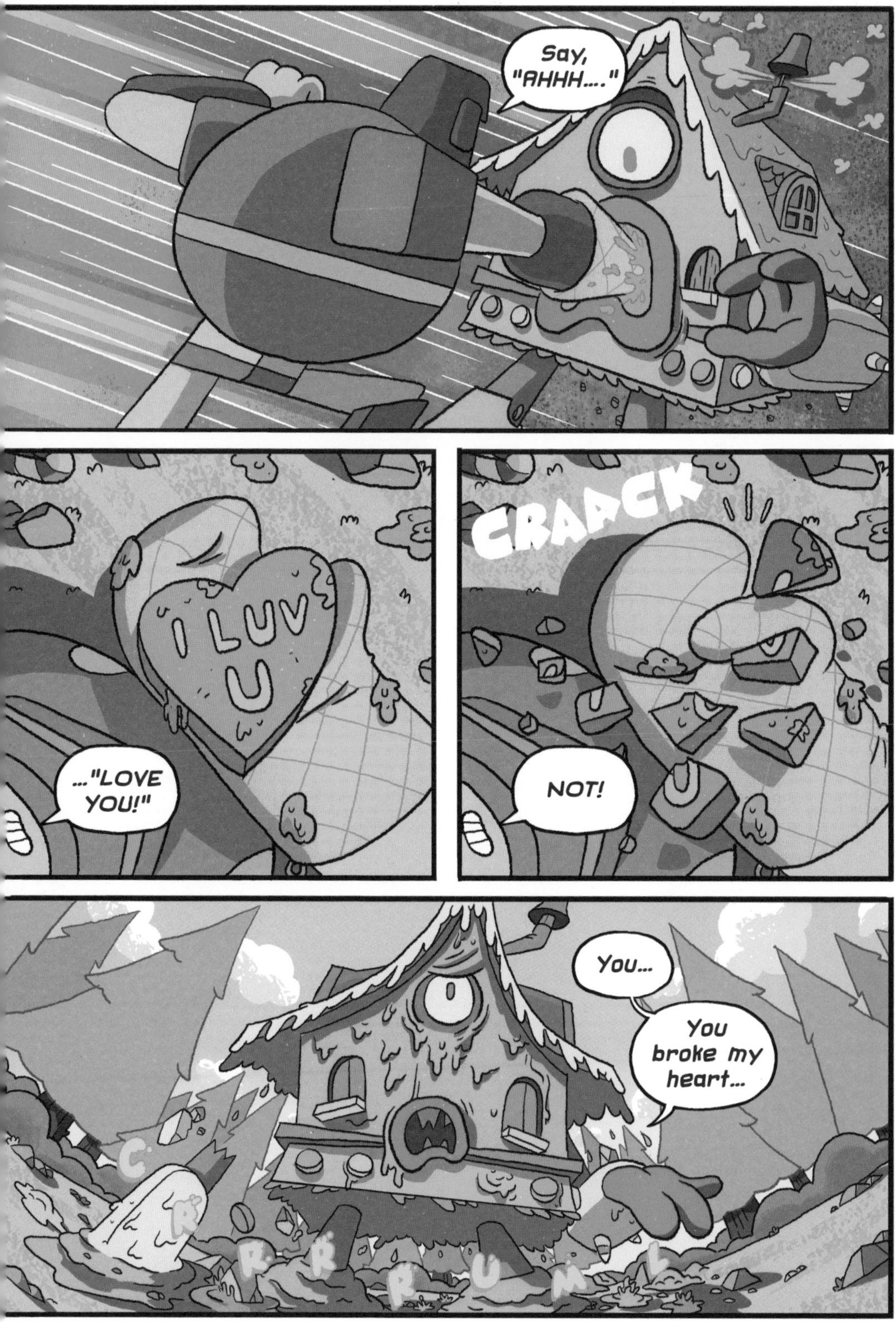
Say, "AHHH...."
I LUV U
..."LOVE YOU!"
CRAACK
NOT!
You...
You broke my heart...
C R R R R U M L

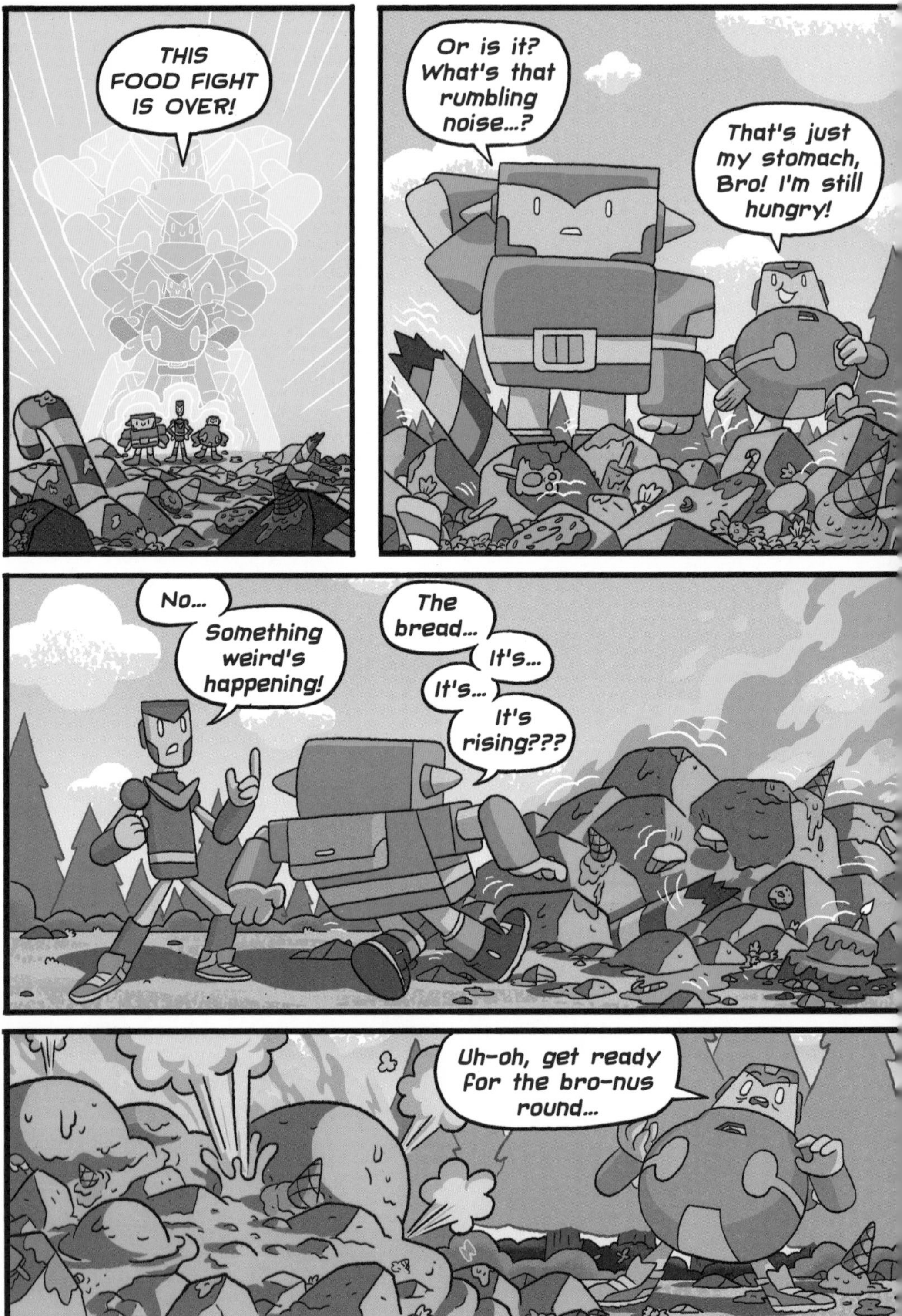
THIS FOOD FIGHT IS OVER!
Or is it? What's that rumbling noise...?
That's just my stomach, Bro! I'm still hungry!
No...
Something weird's happening!
The bread...
It's...
It's...
It's rising???
Uh-oh, get ready for the bro-nus round...

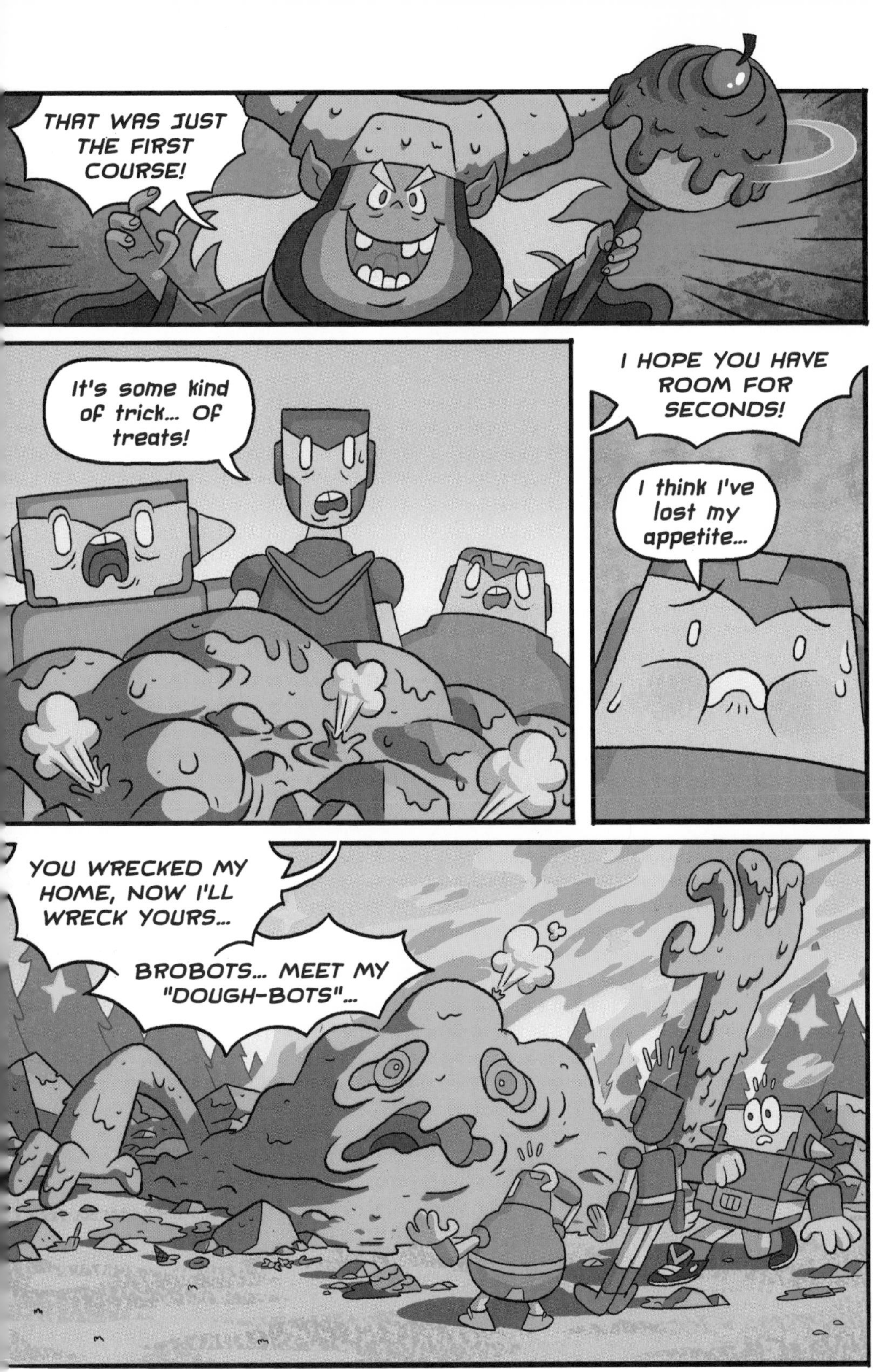
THAT WAS JUST THE FIRST COURSE!
It's some kind of trick... Of treats!
I HOPE YOU HAVE ROOM FOR SECONDS!
I think I've lost my appetite...
YOU WRECKED MY HOME, NOW I'LL WRECK YOURS...
BROBOTS... MEET MY "DOUGH-BOTS"...

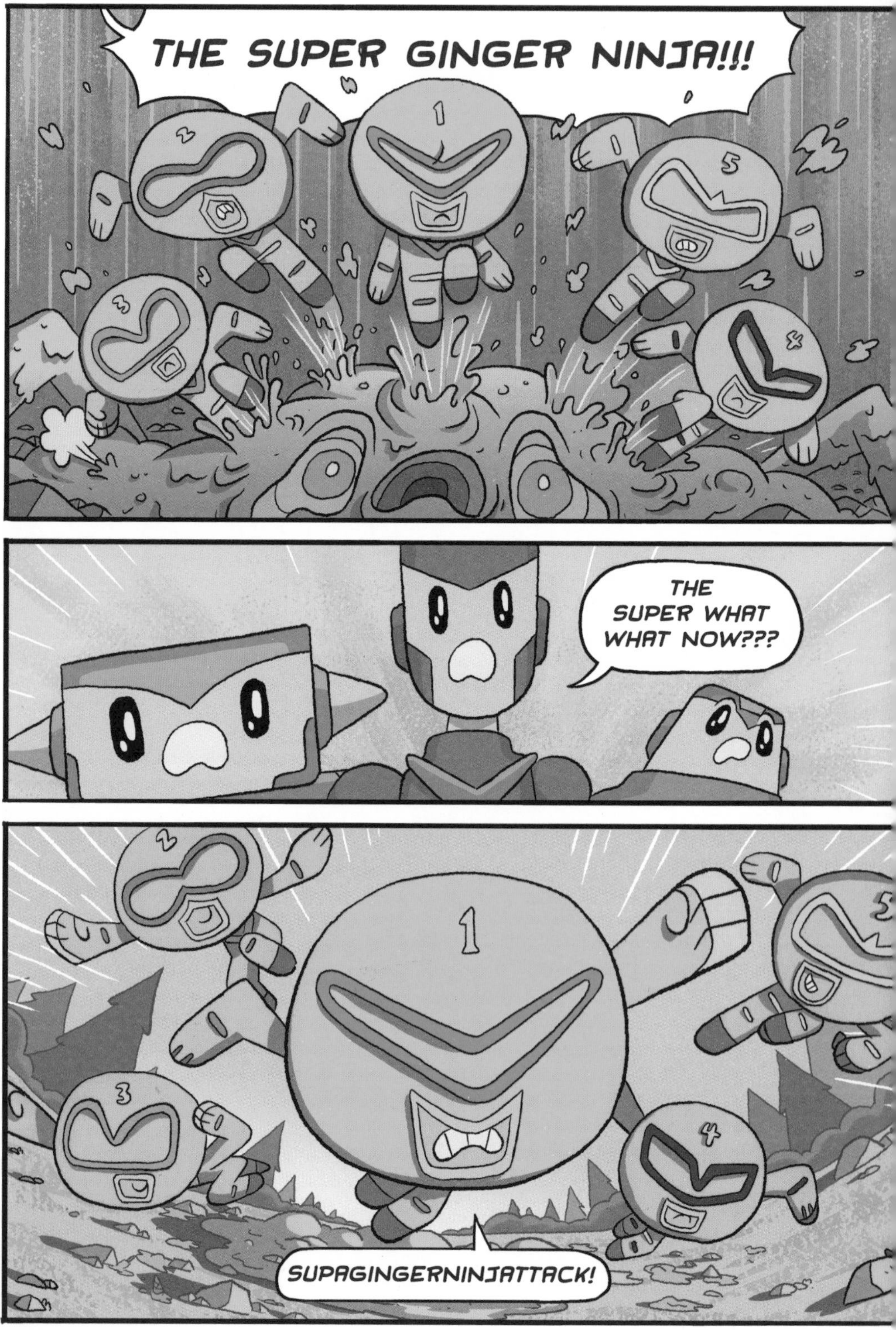
THE SUPER GINGER NINJA!!!
THE SUPER WHAT WHAT NOW???
SUPAGINGERNINJATTACK!

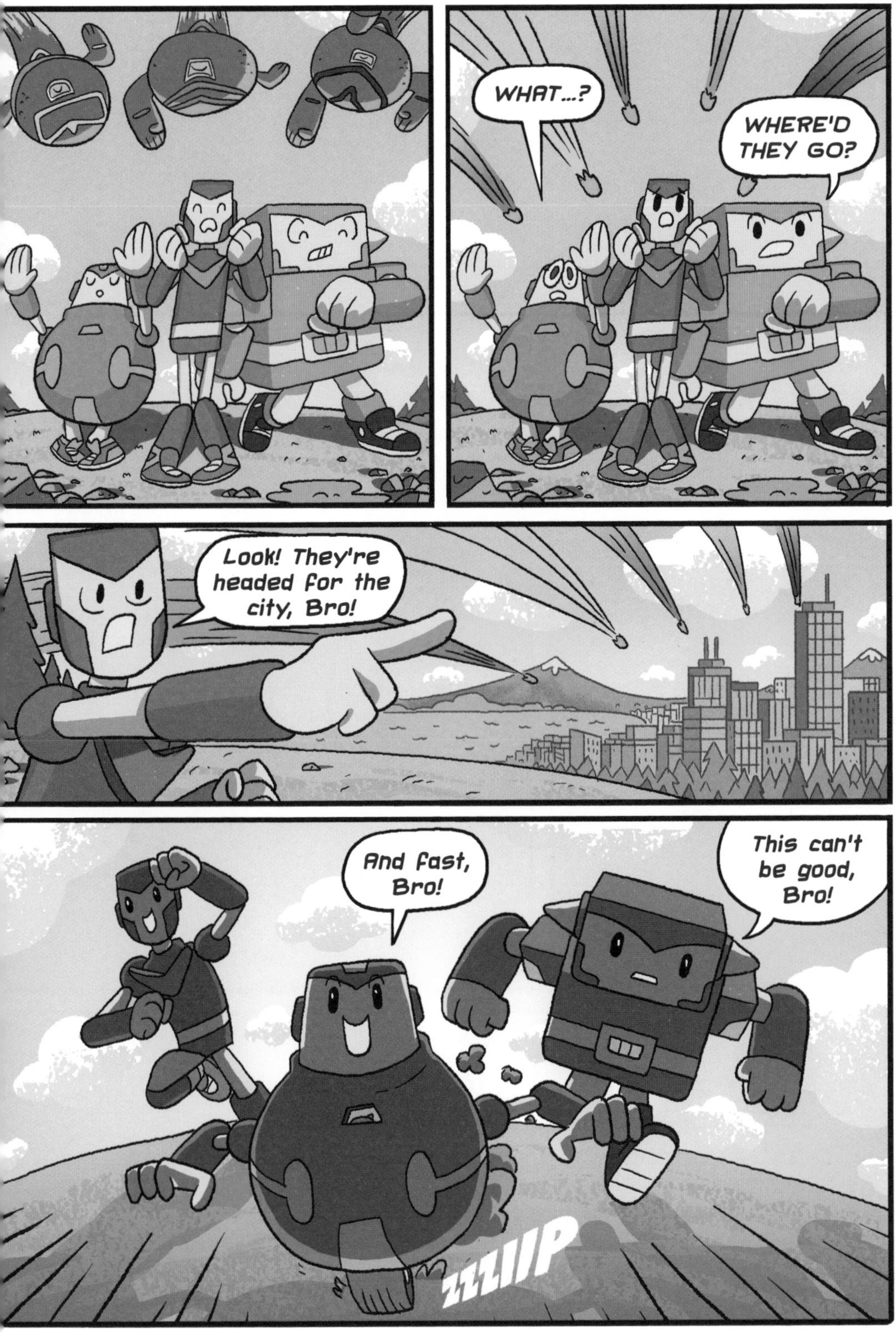
WHAT...?
WHERE'D THEY GO?
Look! They're headed for the city, Bro!
And fast, Bro!
This can't be good, Bro!
ZZZIIIP

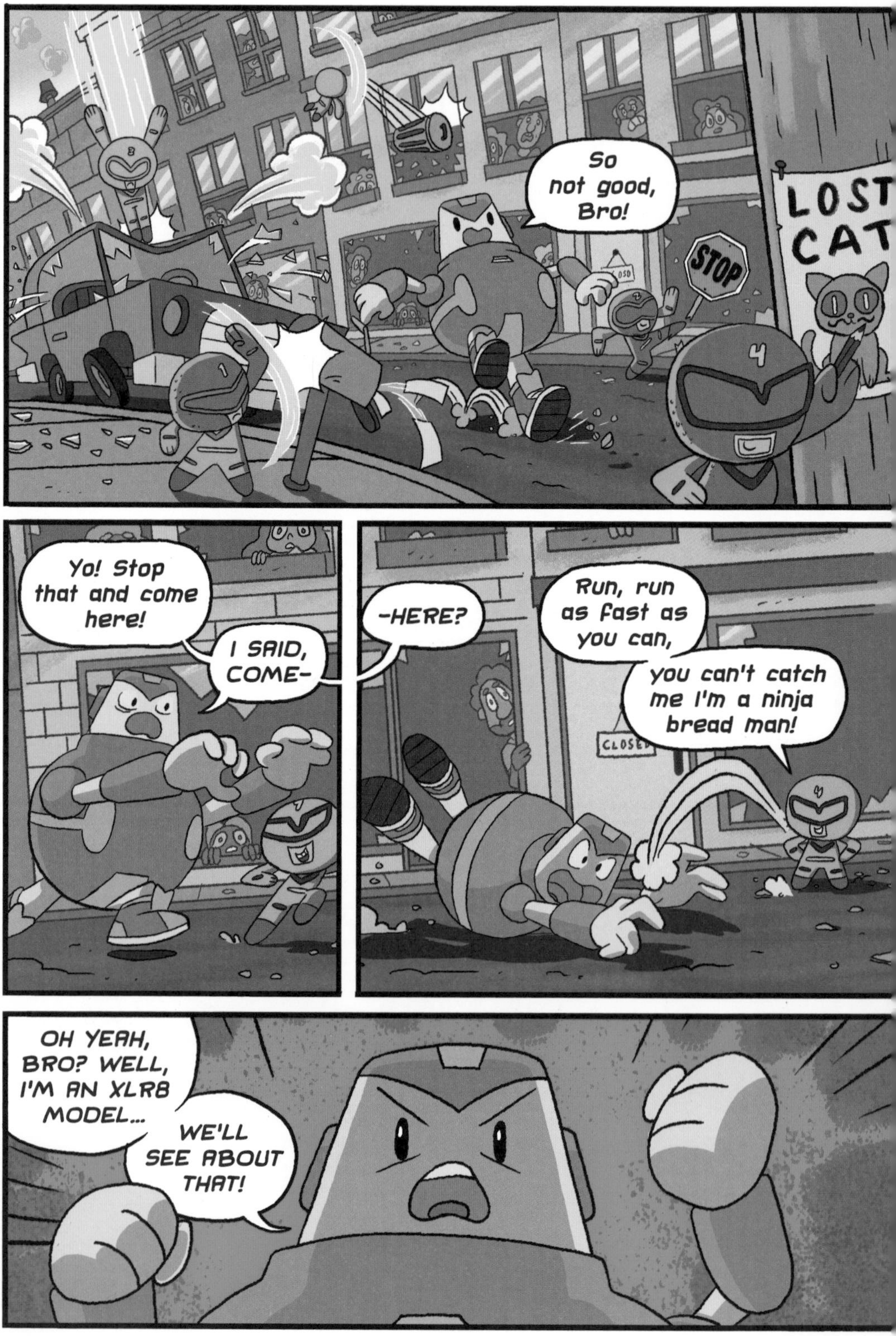
So not good, Bro!
LOST CAT
STOP
Yo! Stop that and come here!
I SAID, COME-
-HERE?
CLOSED
Run, run as fast as you can,
you can't catch me I'm a ninja bread man!
OH YEAH, BRO? WELL, I'M AN XLR8 MODEL...
WE'LL SEE ABOUT THAT!

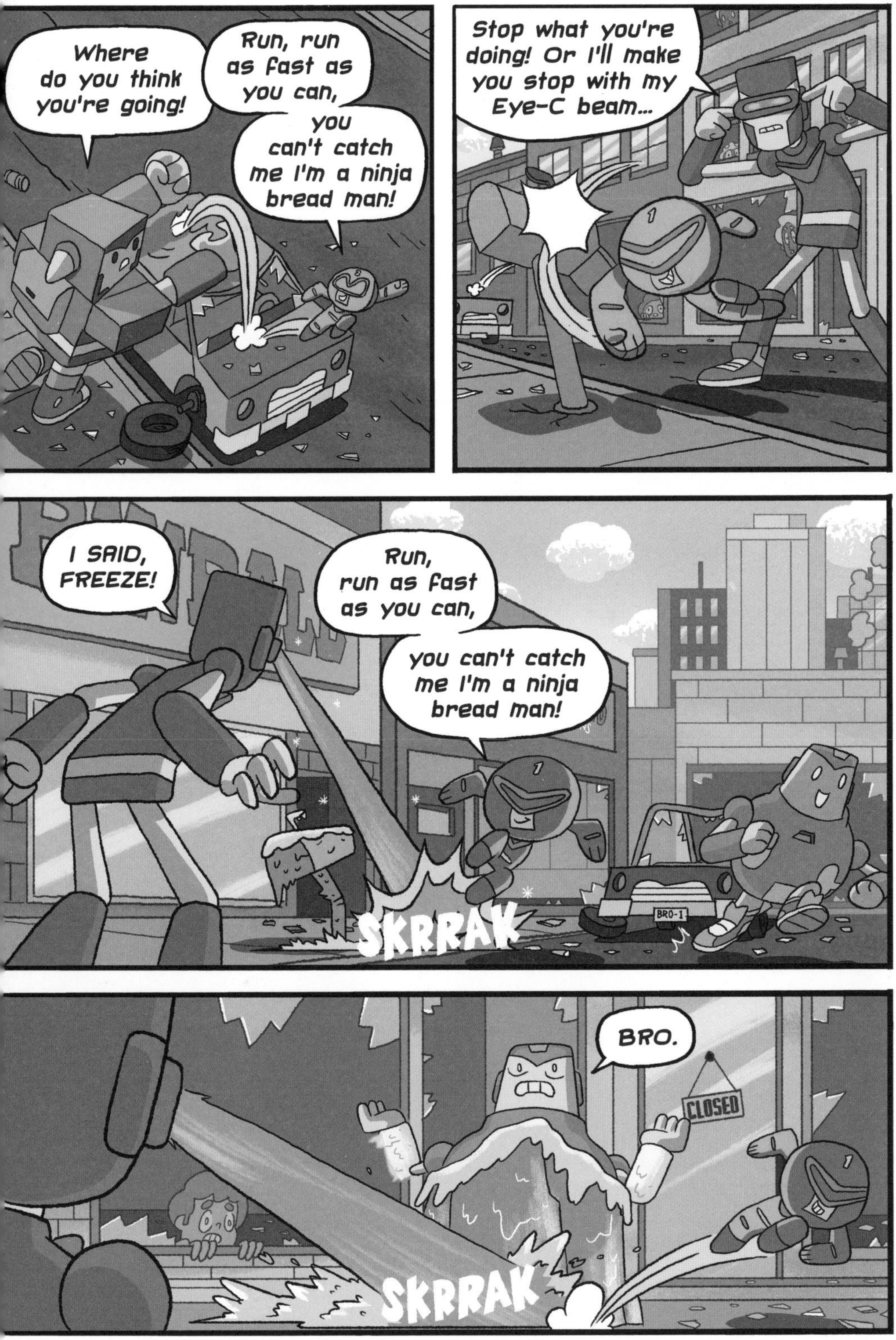
Where do you think you're going!
Run, run as fast as you can,
you can't catch me I'm a ninja bread man!
Stop what you're doing! Or I'll make you stop with my Eye-C beam...
I SAID, FREEZE!
Run, run as fast as you can,
you can't catch me I'm a ninja bread man!
SKRRAK
BRO-1
BRO.
CLOSED
SKRRAK

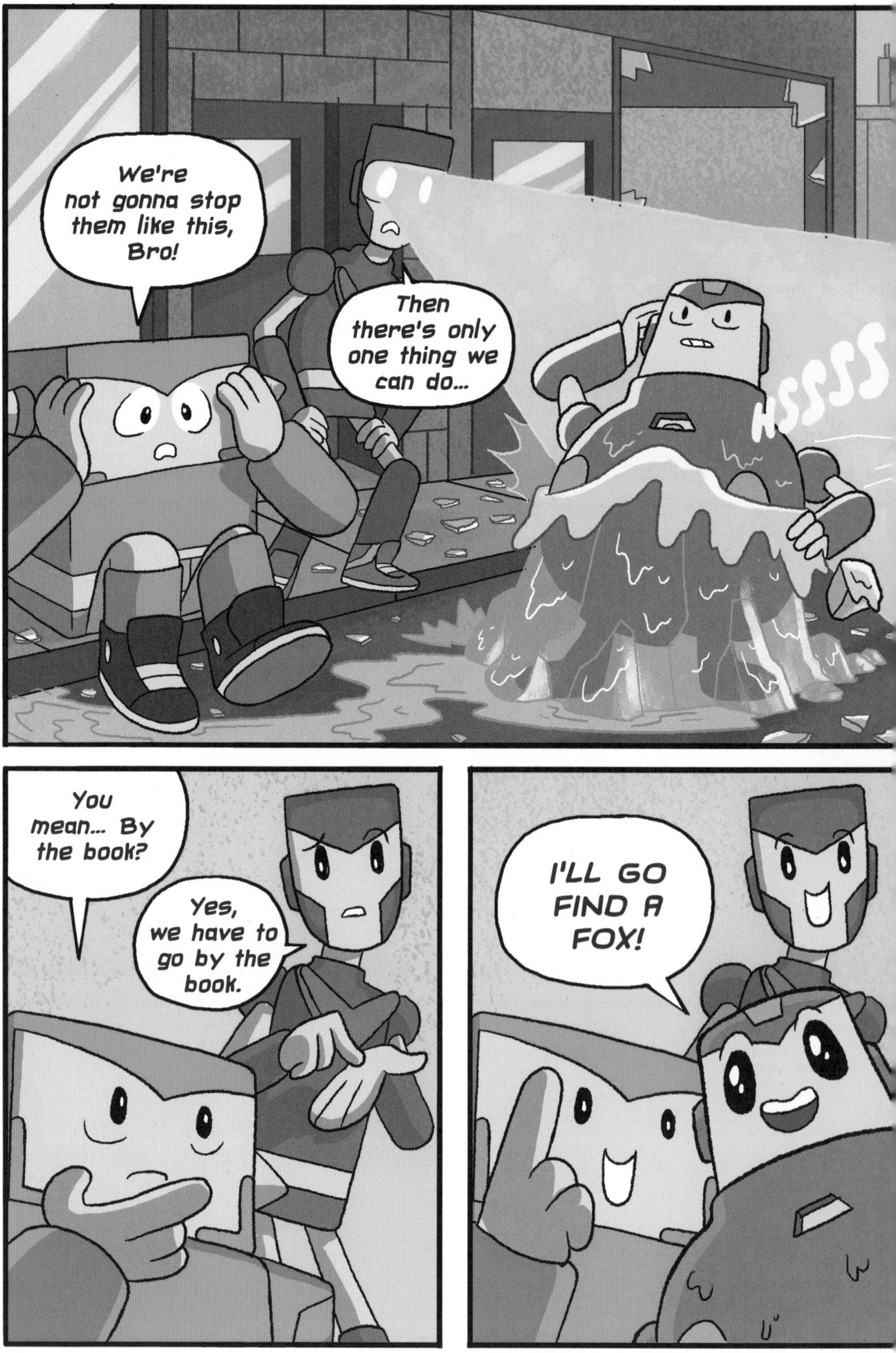
We're not gonna stop them like this, Bro!
Then there's only one thing we can do...
HSSSS
You mean... By the book?
Yes, we have to go by the book.
I'LL GO FIND A FOX!

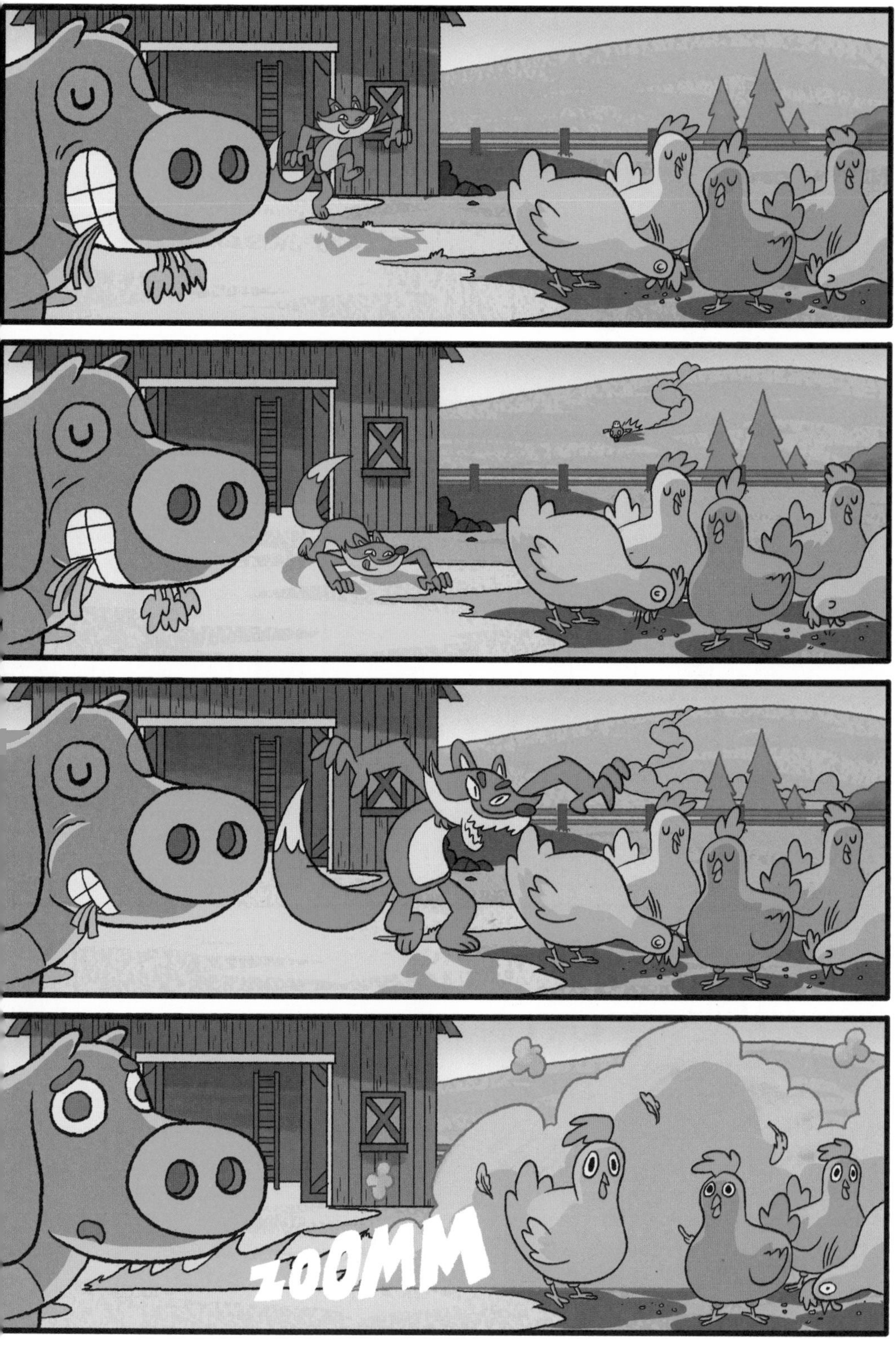
ZOOMM

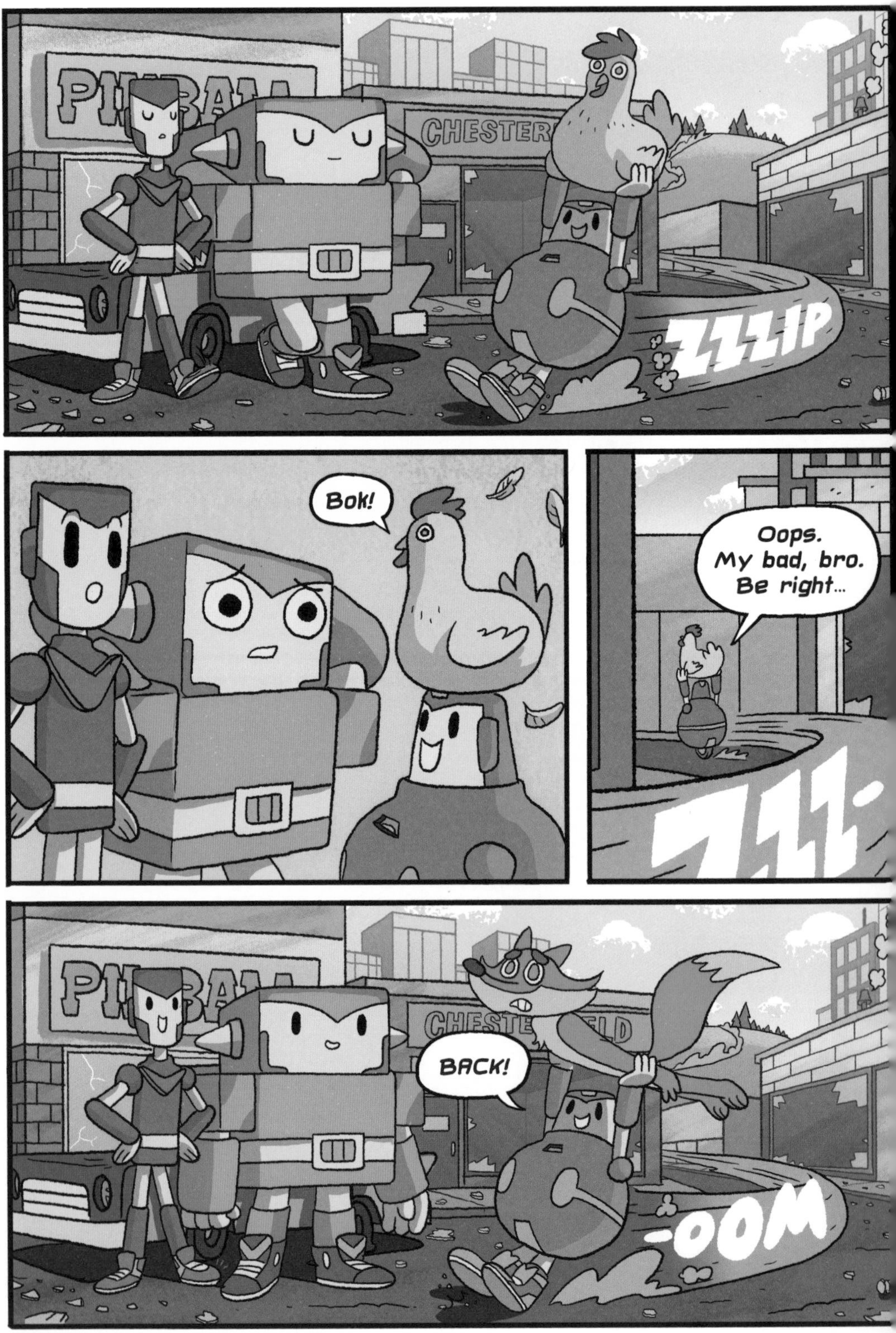
PINBALL
CHESTER
ZZZIP
Bok!
Oops.
My bad, bro.
Be right...
ZZZ-
CHESTERFIELD
BACK!
-OOM

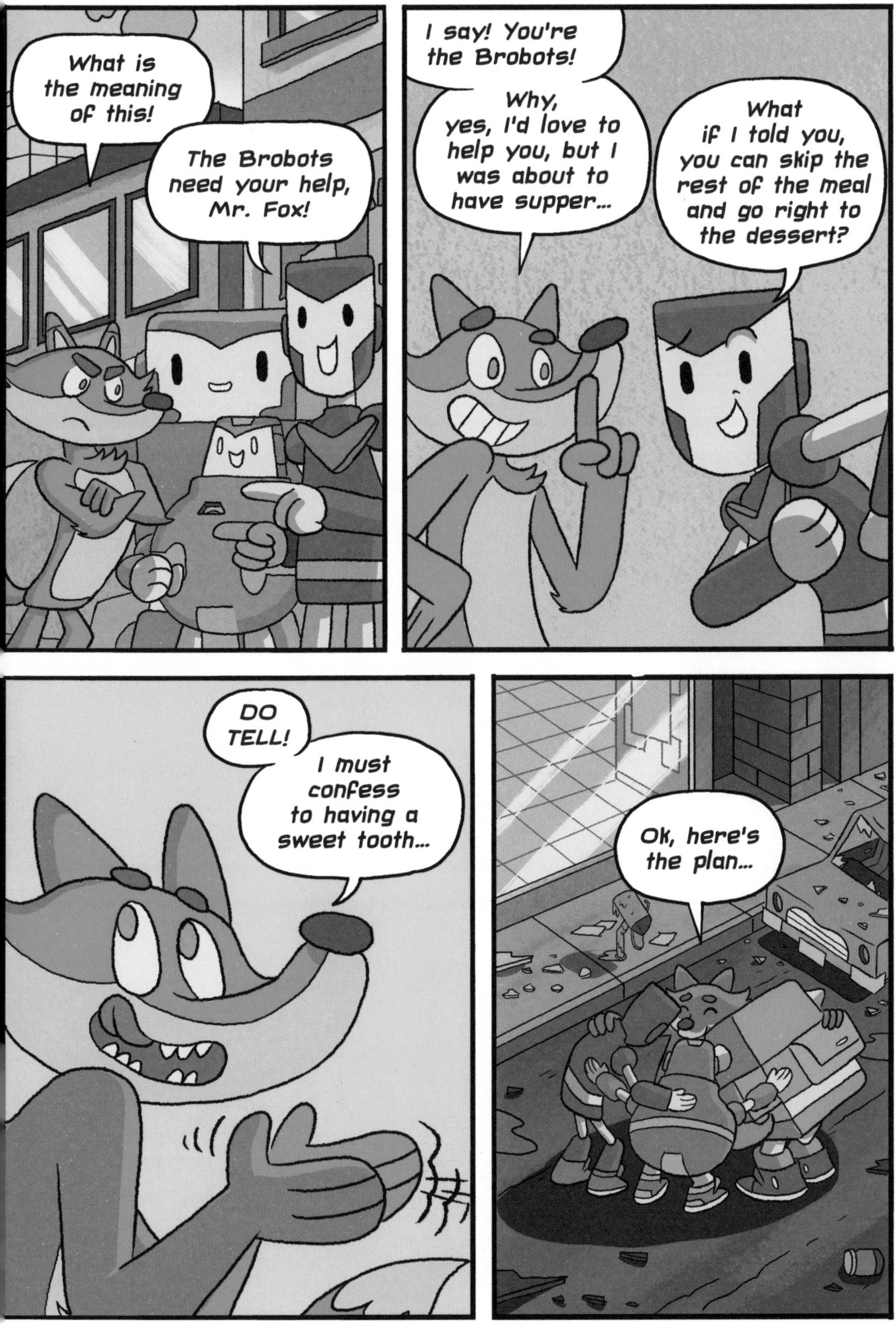
What is the meaning of this!
The Brobots need your help, Mr. Fox!
I say! You're the Brobots!
Why, yes, I'd love to help you, but I was about to have supper...
What if I told you, you can skip the rest of the meal and go right to the dessert?
DO TELL!
I must confess to having a sweet tooth...
Ok, here's the plan...

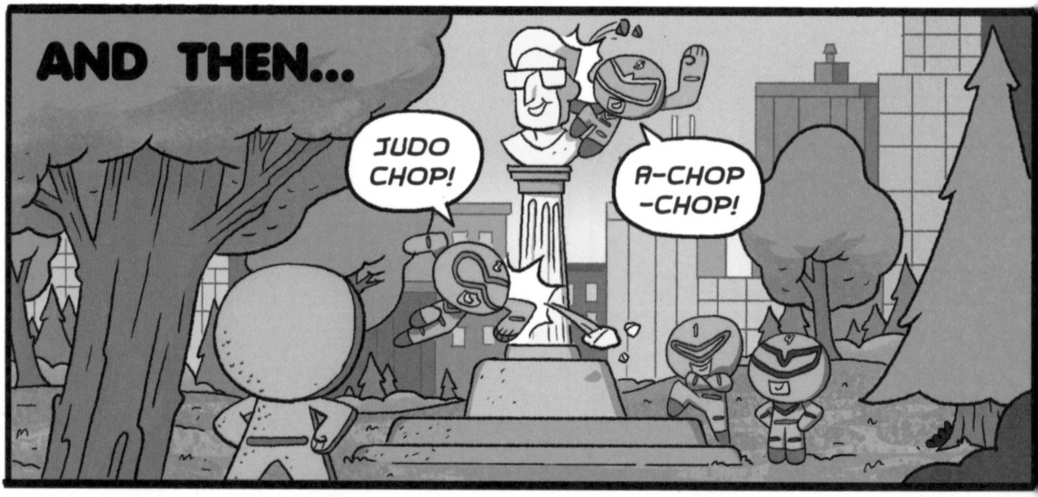
AND THEN...
JUDO CHOP!
A-CHOP -CHOP!

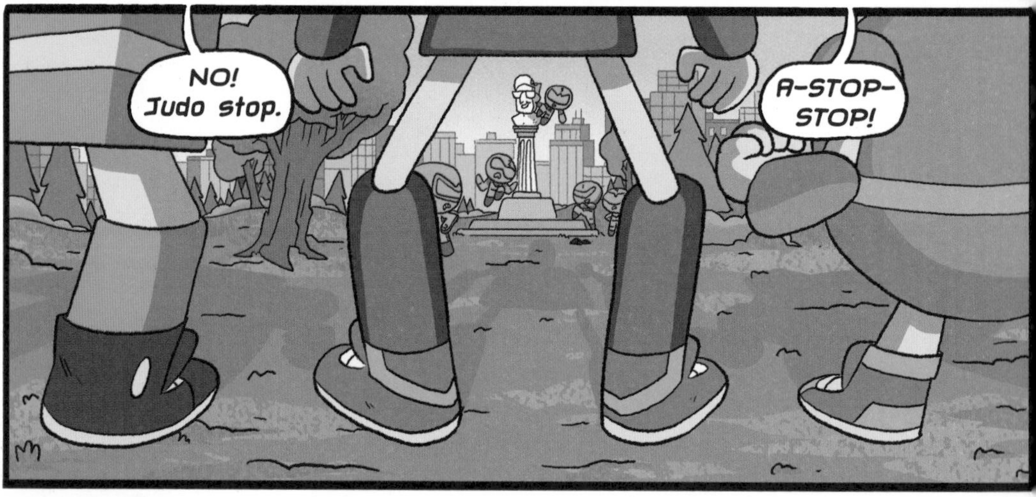
NO! Judo stop.
A-STOP-STOP!

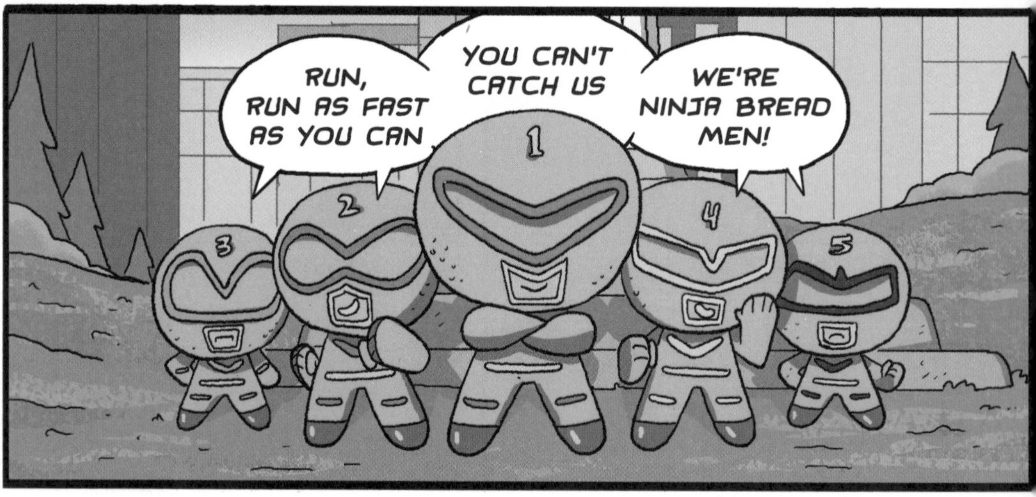
RUN, RUN AS FAST AS YOU CAN
YOU CAN'T CATCH US
WE'RE NINJA BREAD MEN!

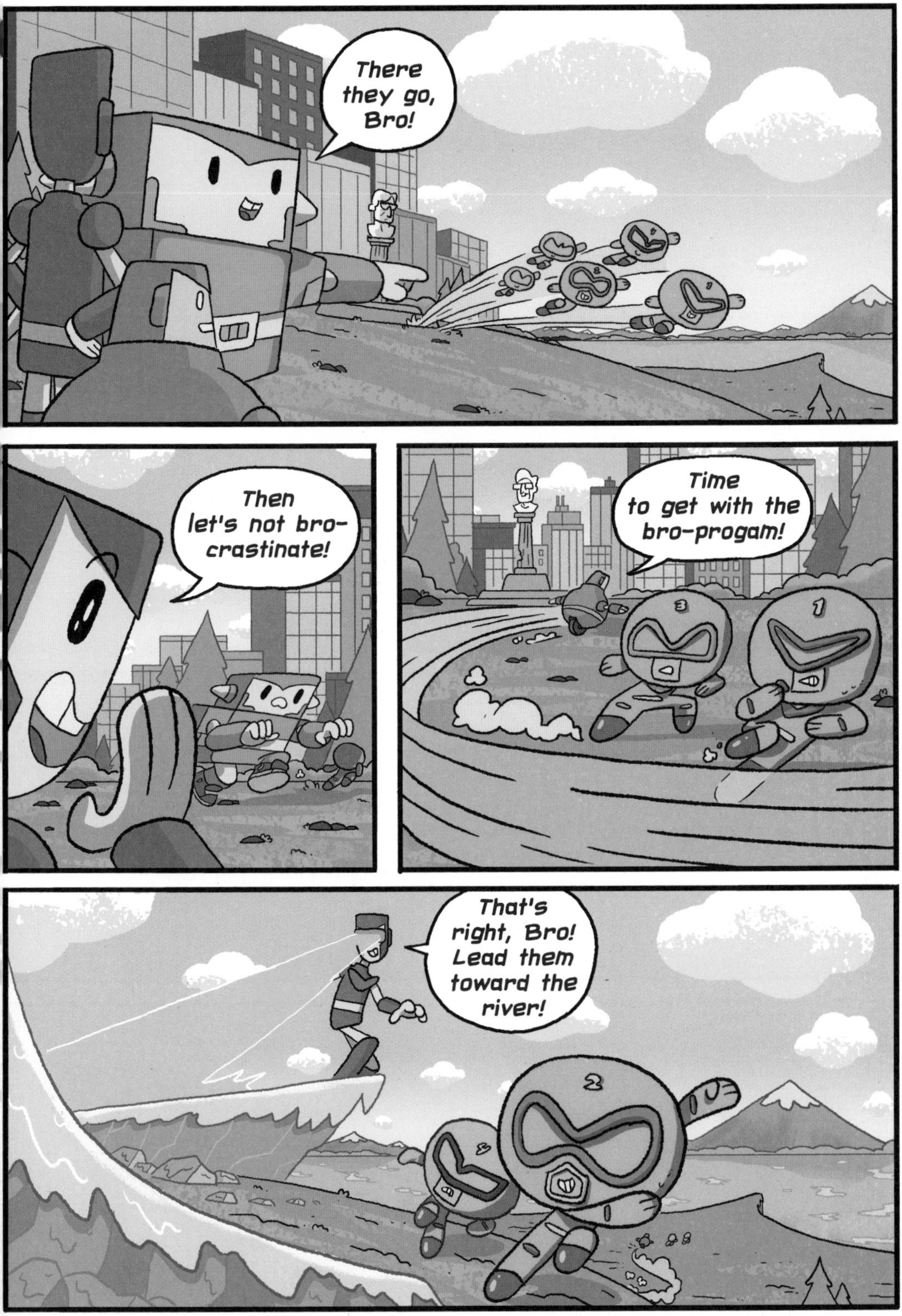
There they go, Bro!
Then let's not bro-crastinate!
Time to get with the bro-progam!
That's right, Bro! Lead them toward the river!

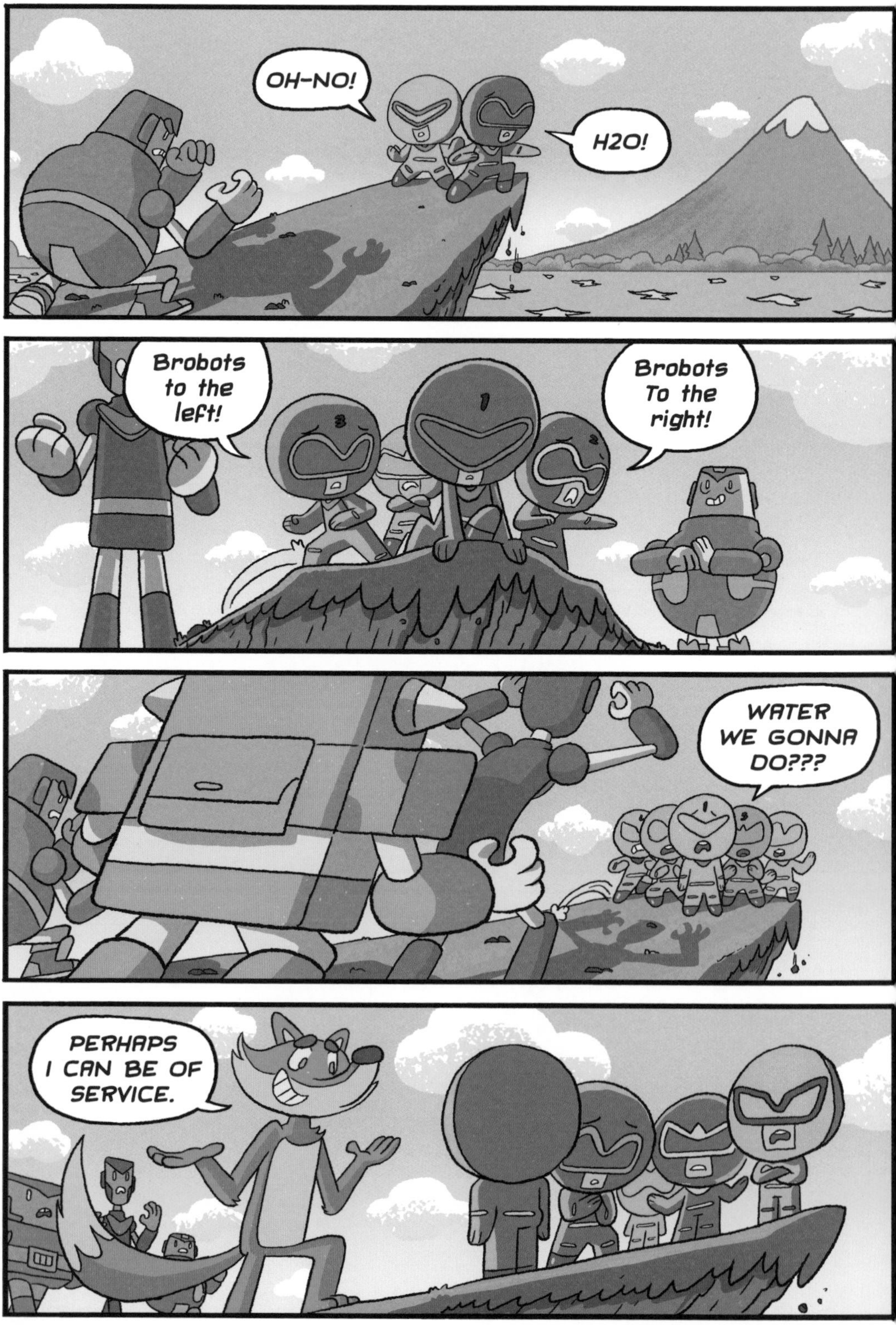
OH-NO!
H2O!
Brobots to the left!
Brobots To the right!
WATER WE GONNA DO???
PERHAPS I CAN BE OF SERVICE.

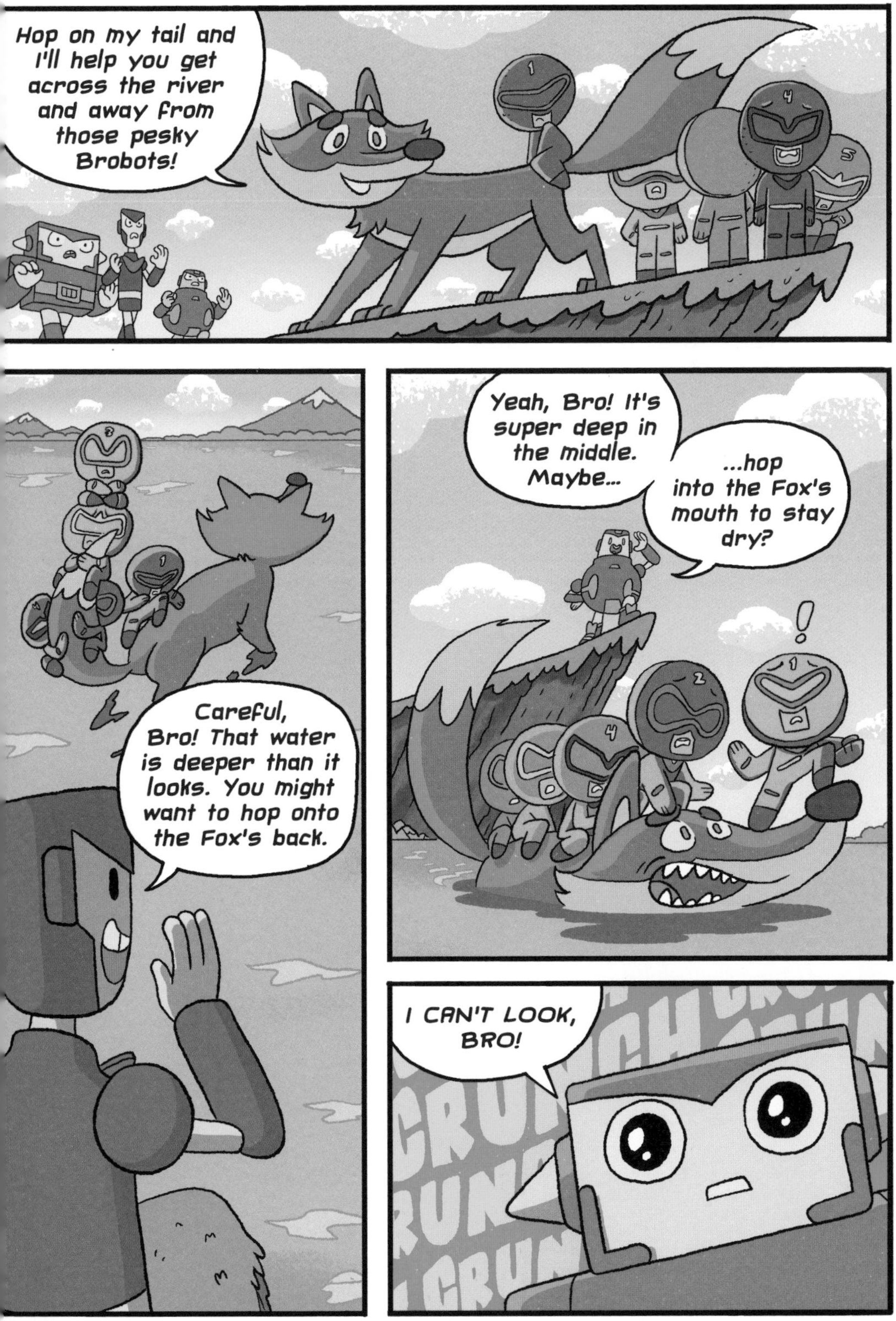

Hop on my tail and I'll help you get across the river and away from those pesky Brobots!
Careful, Bro! That water is deeper than it looks. You might want to hop onto the Fox's back.
Yeah, Bro! It's super deep in the middle. Maybe...
...hop into the Fox's mouth to stay dry?
!
I CAN'T LOOK, BRO!
CRUNCH

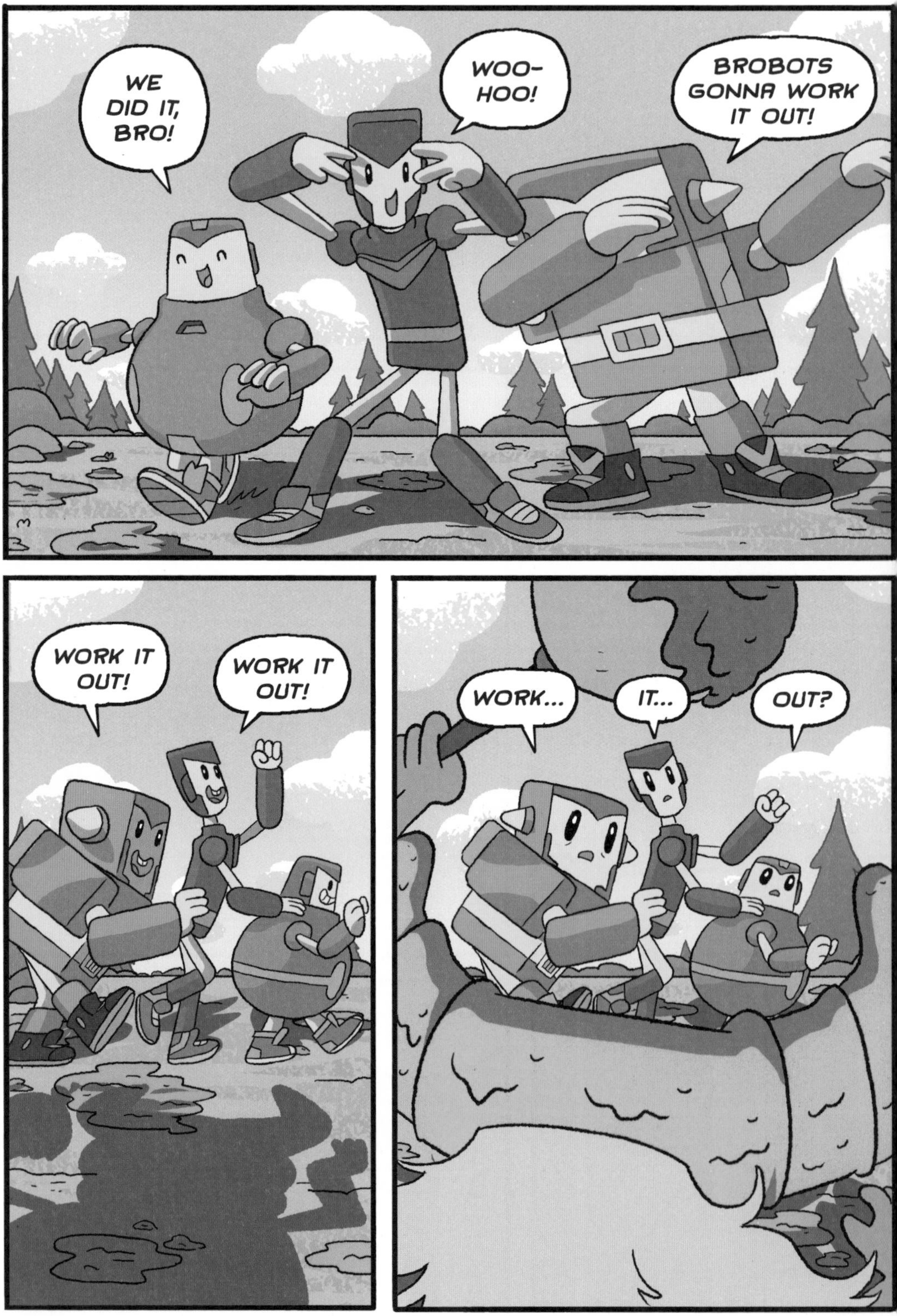
WE DID IT, BRO!
WOO-HOO!
BROBOTS GONNA WORK IT OUT!
WORK IT OUT!
WORK IT OUT!
WORK...
IT...
OUT?

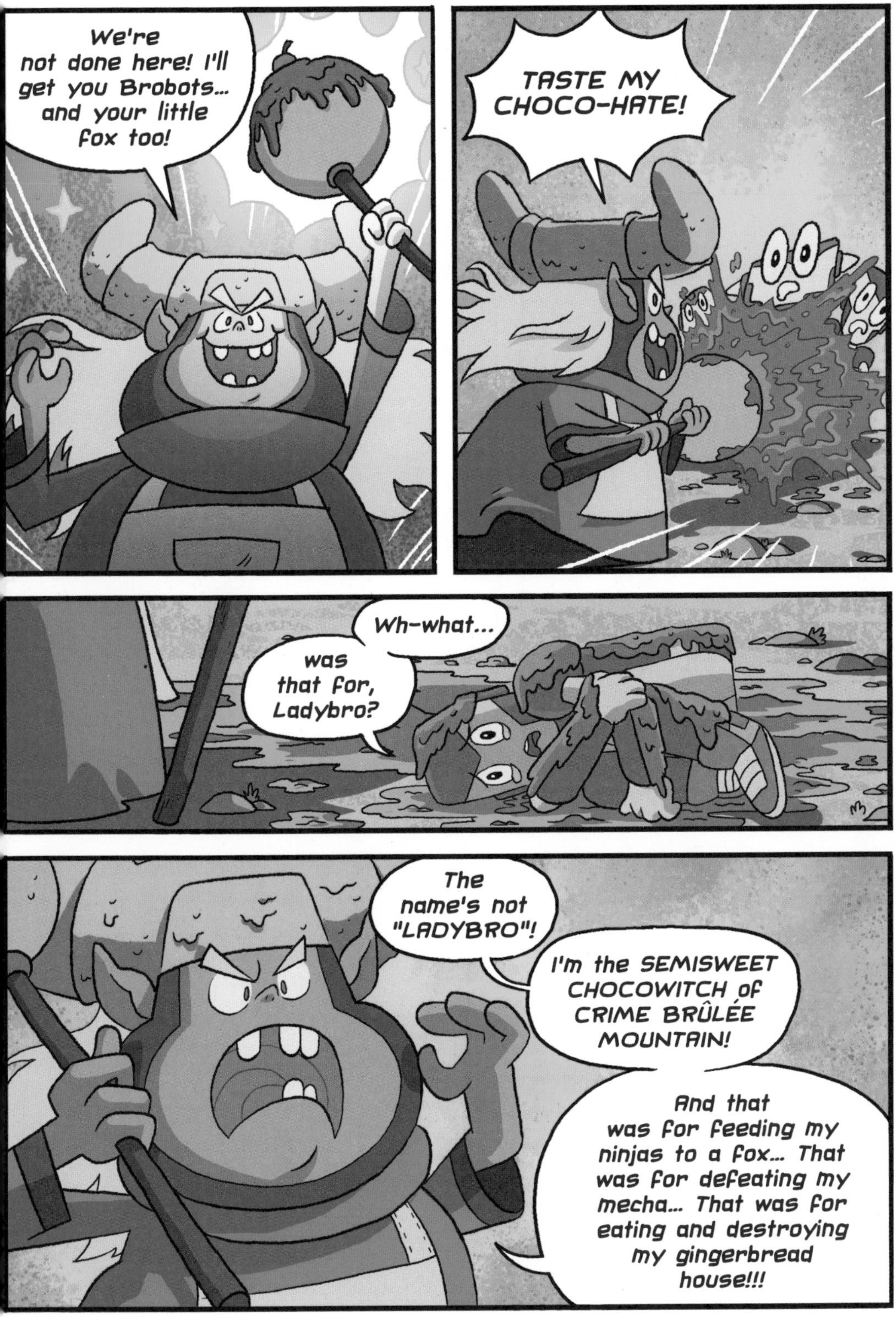

We're not done here! I'll get you Brobots... and your little fox too!
TASTE MY CHOCO-HATE!
Wh-what...
was that for, Ladybro?
The name's not "LADYBRO"!
I'm the SEMISWEET CHOCOWITCH of CRIME BRÛLÉE MOUNTAIN!
And that was for feeding my ninjas to a fox... That was for defeating my mecha... That was for eating and destroying my gingerbread house!!!

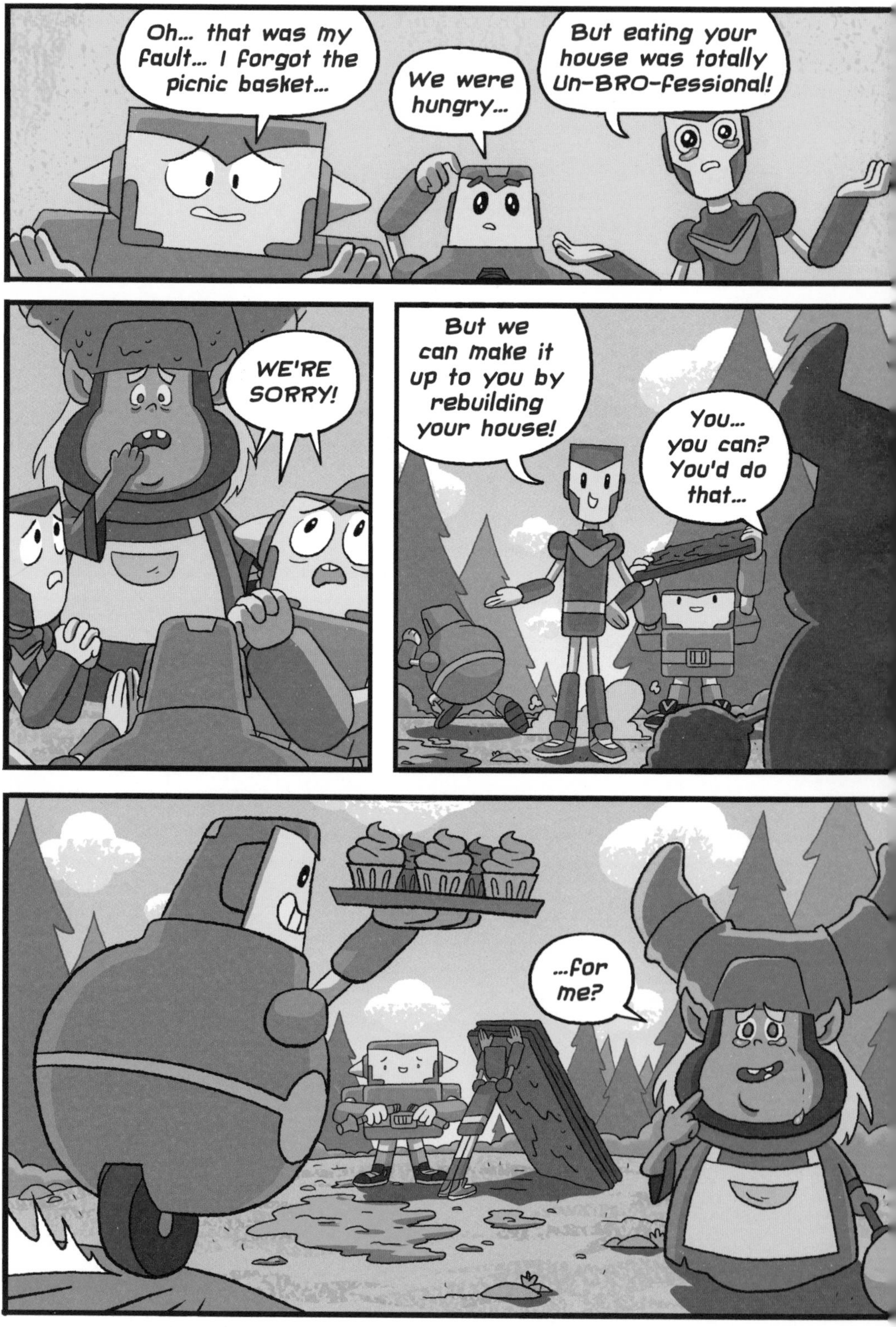
Oh... that was my fault... I forgot the picnic basket...
We were hungry...
But eating your house was totally Un-BRO-fessional!
WE'RE SORRY!
But we can make it up to you by rebuilding your house!
You... you can? You'd do that...
...for me?

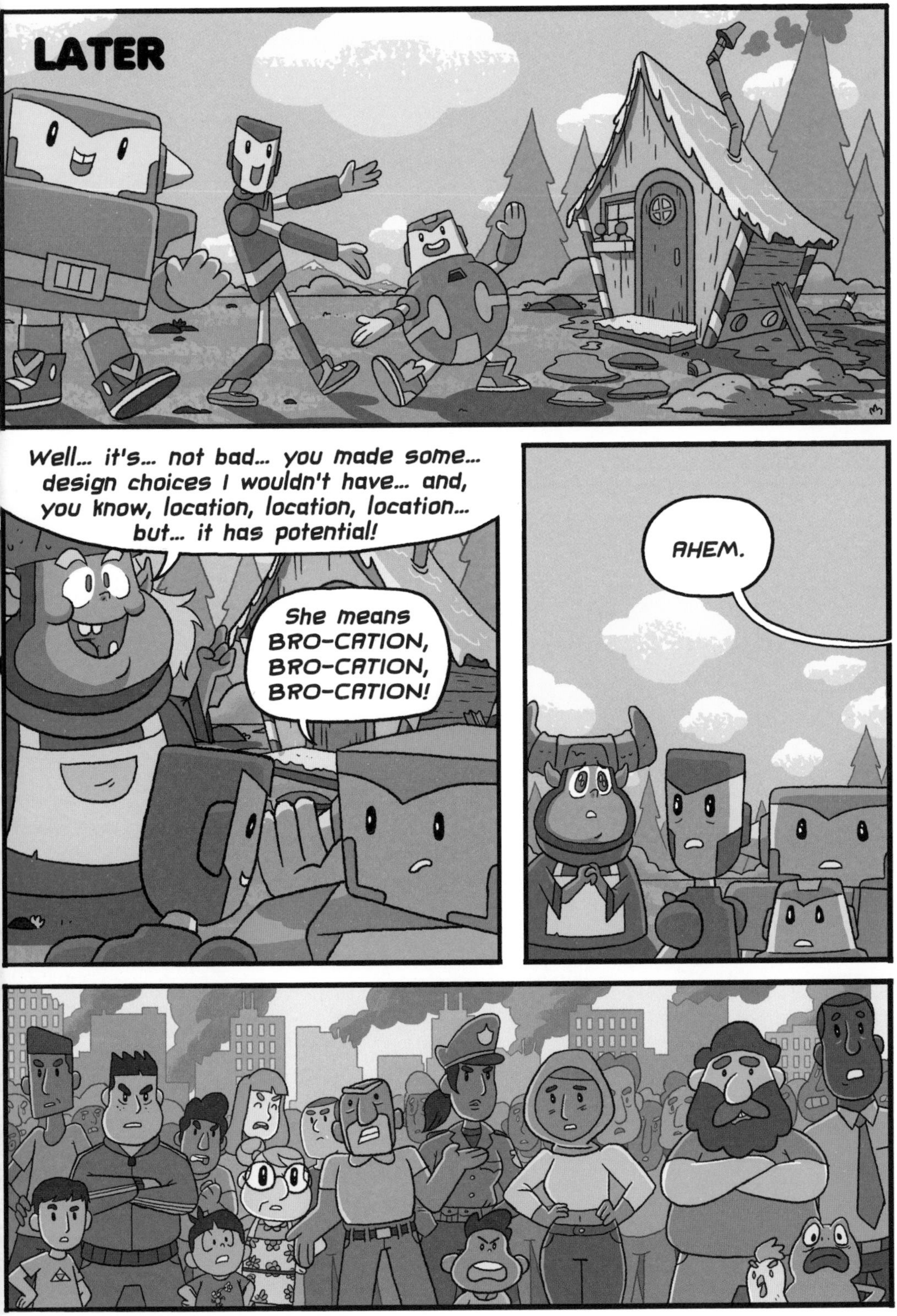
LATER
Well... it's... not bad... you made some... design choices I wouldn't have... and, you know, location, location, location... but... it has potential!
She means BRO-CATION, BRO-CATION, BRO-CATION!
AHEM.

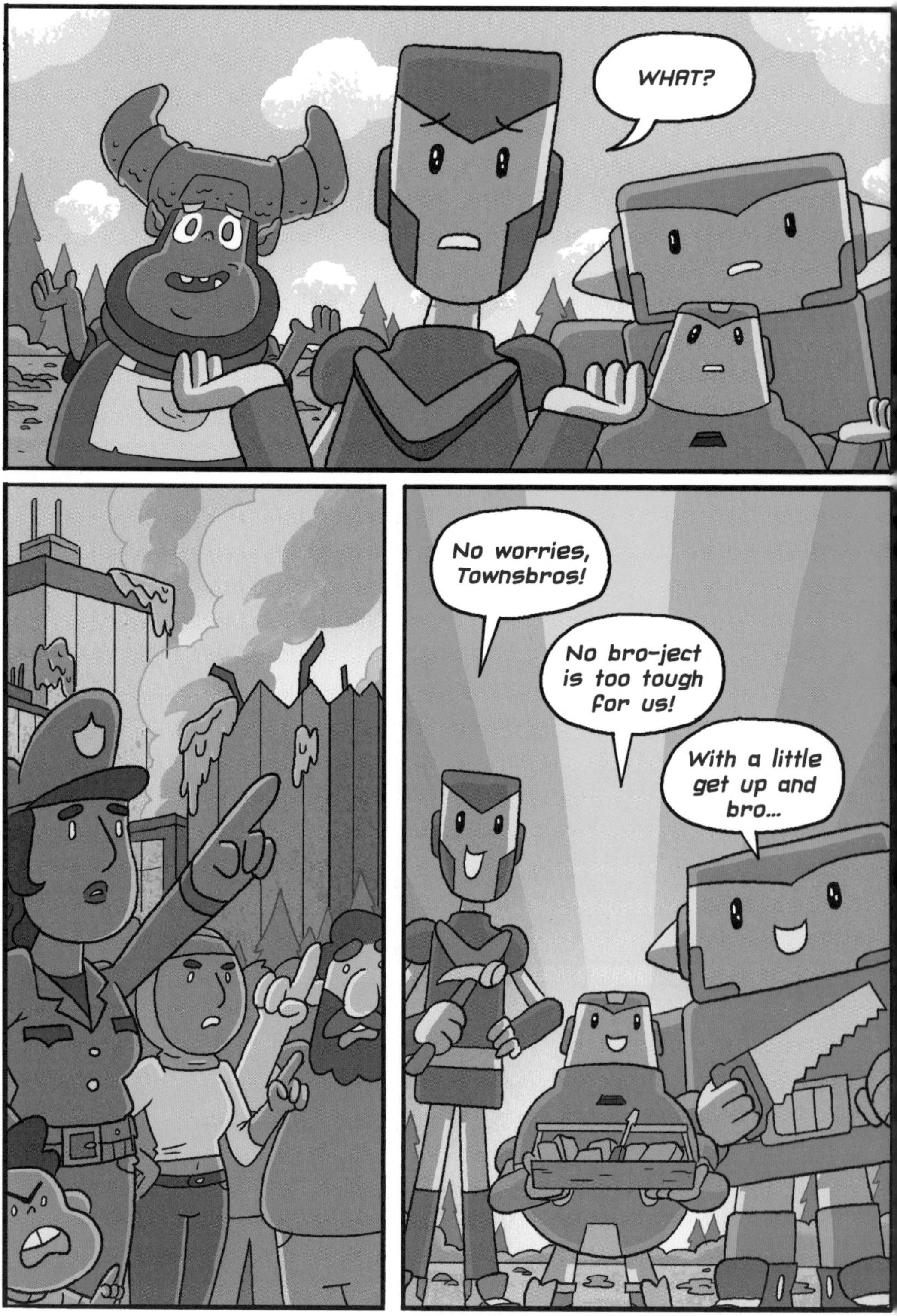
WHAT?
No worries, Townsbros!
No bro-ject is too tough for us!
With a little get up and bro...

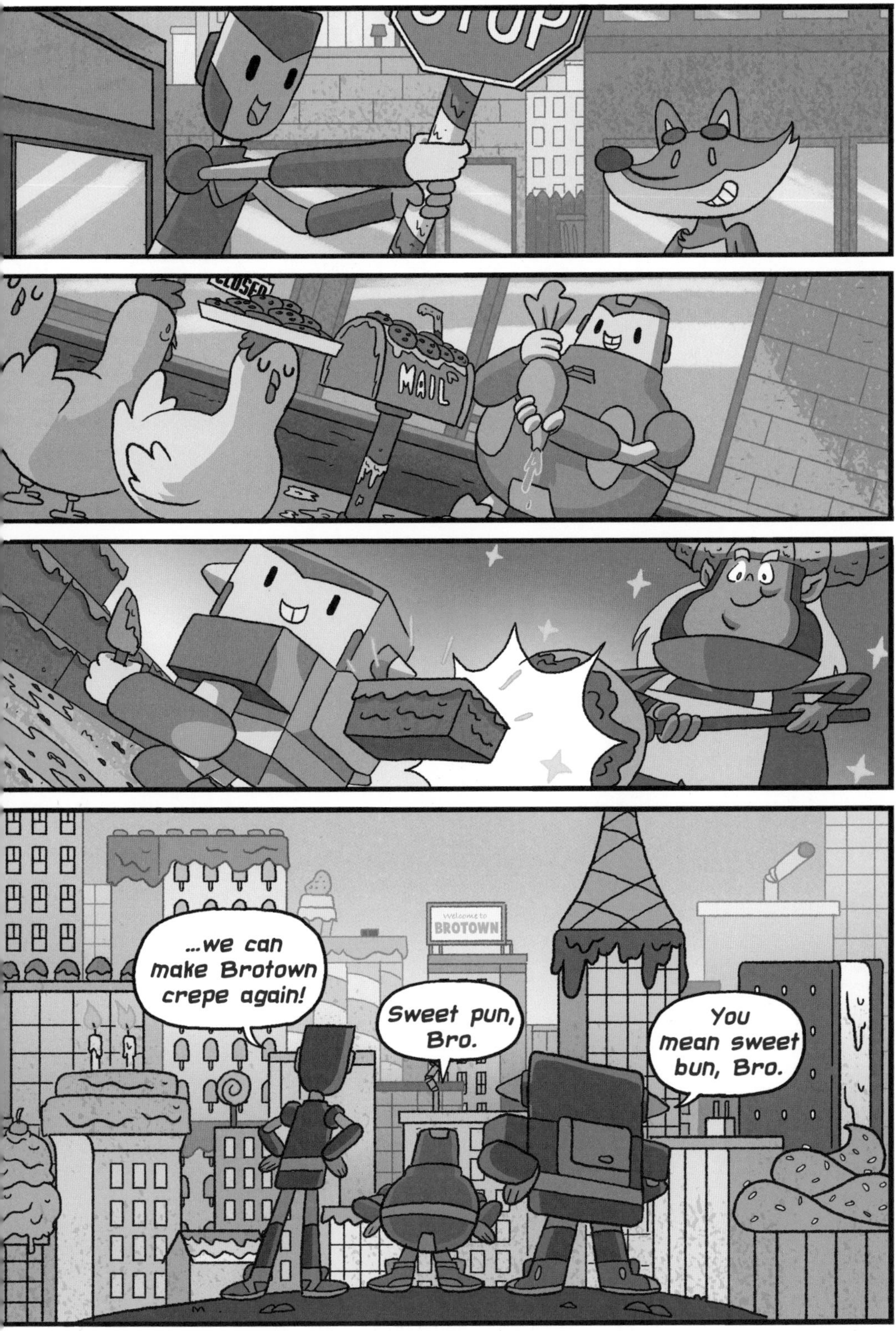
MAIL
Welcome to
BROTOWN
...we can make Brotown crepe again!
Sweet pun, Bro.
You mean sweet bun, Bro.

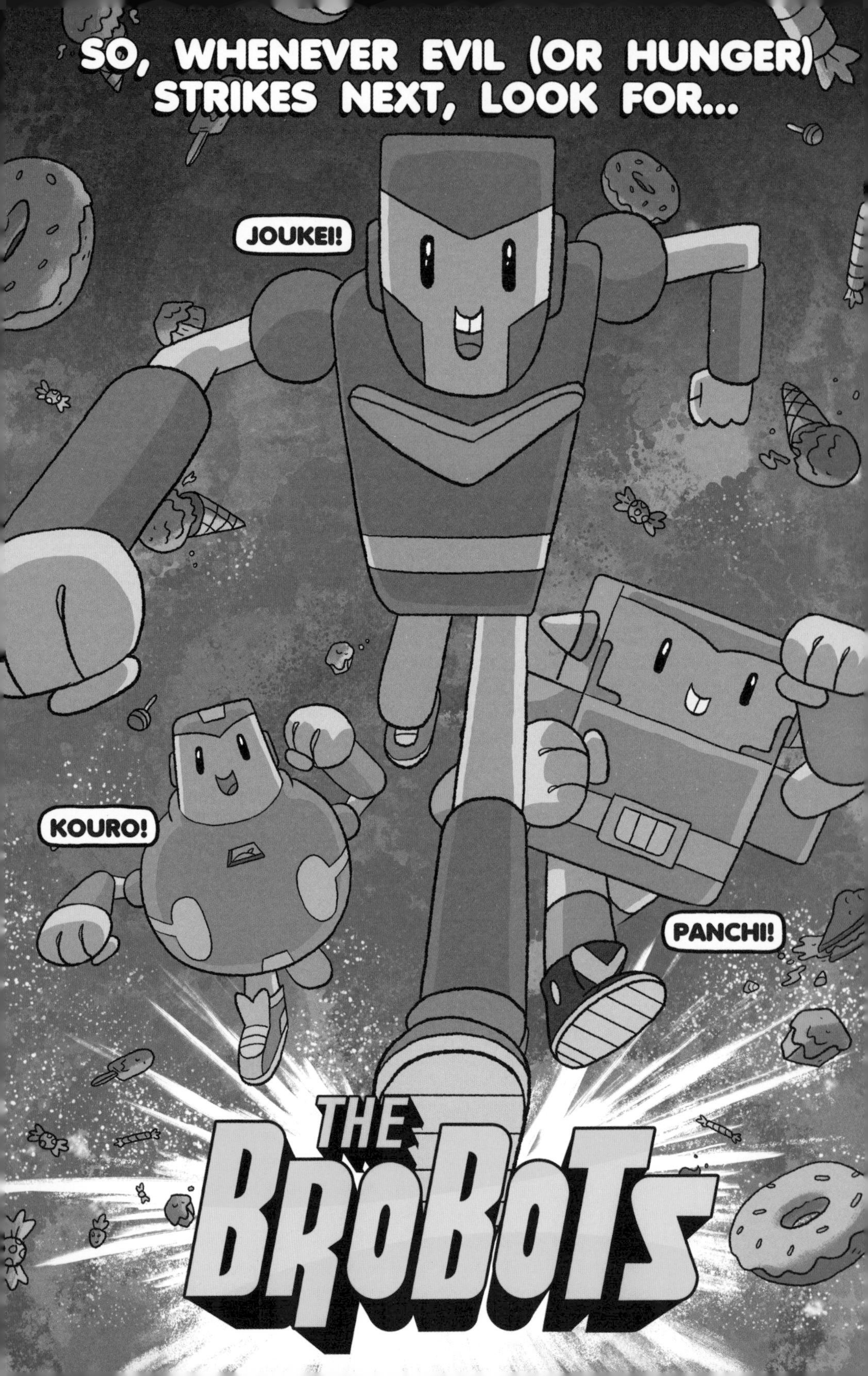
SO, WHENEVER EVIL (OR HUNGER) STRIKES NEXT, LOOK FOR...
JOUKEI!
KOURO!
PANCHI!
THE BROBOTS

About The Authors

J. TORRES

J. Torres is a comic book writer who lives just outside Toronto, Canada. His other credits include *Alison Dare, Bigfoot Boy, Do-Gooders, Lola: A Ghost Story, Power Lunch, The Mighty Zodiac,* and *Teen Titans Go.*

His favourite sweet treats include black sesame ice cream, casaba cake, cheesecake, coconut milk tea boba, and chocolate covered macadamia nuts.

J. would like to dedicate this book to his sons Pie-sander and Tart-tus.

SEAN DOVE

Sean lives and works in Chicago, IL where he runs his one-man design and illustration studio And Thank You For Flying. Sean self-published *The Last Days of Danger*, worked on *Madballs*, and draws his comic series *Fried Rice*.

His favourite sweet treats include carrot cake, chocolate chip cookies, botan rice candy, Snickers and anything chocloate.

Sean would like to thank his parents, Rose and 4 Star Studios.